Praise for the work of Vonna Harper

"*Shifters' Storm* is a moving, erotic and evocative love story set against the incredible beauty of the Chinook Mountains in winter. Highly recommended."

~ *Whipped Cream Reviews*

"*Shifters' Storm* is not for the faint at heart, the powerful emotions emanating from each of these characters is shared in vivid detail. I was immediately drawn into this book and enjoyed every minute I spent with the characters."

~ *Fresh Fiction*

Look for these titles by
Vonna Harper

Now Available:

Bloodhunter
Predator
Night Hunter
Shifters' Storm
Studs

Night Hunter

Vonna Harper

Samhain Publishing, Ltd.
11821 Mason Montgomery Road, 4B
Cincinnati, OH 45249
www.samhainpublishing.com

Night Hunter
Copyright © 2012 by Vonna Harper
Print ISBN: 978-1-60928-440-4
Digital ISBN: 978-1-60928-418-3

Editing by Linda Ingmanson
Cover by Kanaxa

This book is a work of fiction. The names, characters, places, and incidents are products of the writer's imagination or have been used fictitiously and are not to be construed as real. Any resemblance to persons, living or dead, actual events, locale or organizations is entirely coincidental.

All Rights Are Reserved. No part of this book may be used or reproduced in any manner whatsoever without written permission, except in the case of brief quotations embodied in critical articles and reviews.

This book has been previously published and has been revised from its original release.

First Samhain Publishing, Ltd. electronic publication: April 2011
First Samhain Publishing, Ltd. print publication: March 2012

Dedication

When my sister-in-law moved from the West coast to Florida, I thought she'd lost her mind. As a lover of mountains and forests, I naïvely thought I'd hate humid Florida. Then my husband and I visited. Granted, the humidity still kicks my butt, but it's an amazing place. I fell in love with the swift and sometimes violent weather swings, the great variety of birds, the bajillion lizards, and even more seashells. "I want to see the Everglades," I declared. Because my sister-in-law and her husband couldn't take the time from work, Dick and I headed across what's called Alligator Alley. I drove, gaping and then gaping some more as the world turned purple and rain came at us sidewise. In true writer fashion, even as I fought to keep the car on the road, the "what ifs" started. What if a man on a black motorcycle locks eyes with a woman one storm-tossed afternoon? What if he loses control and slides into the Everglades? What if, when the woman goes looking for him, he isn't there?

So Mern, this one's for you. I couldn't love you more if we shared the same genetics. Thanks for giving me a reason to call Florida the home of my heart.

Chapter One

The storm flung itself at Mala Bey's car. Attacking, sometimes shrieking, it buffeted her small vehicle until Mala was forced to slow to thirty miles an hour. Her windshield wipers were all but useless.

Blue-black, the cloud-choked sky dominated everything. Occasionally, Mala glimpsed a sliver of gold on the horizon which gave her hope that the entire world wasn't locked in this furious Florida afternoon storm, but she had little time to reflect on anything except making sure she didn't skid off the highway and plunge into the Everglades lurking on either side.

Alligator Alley. If she got out of this alive, she'd get in touch with whoever was responsible for naming highways and tell them they hadn't gotten it right. This too-thin thread of civilization cutting east to west through southern Florida should go by something like *Hell's Back Yard. Dark Deception. Thunder*—

Crack!

The explosion worked in harmony with the fingers of brilliant light erupting on the sky. As a native of a state regularly attacked by violent weather, she should be used to the power and overwhelming energy. But, except for a handful of vehicles plowing through the deluge, she was alone in a savage and primal land. The storm wouldn't last long, and the sun would return to bake and steam the earth. She should have waited to travel from Naples to Fort Lauderdale, but a huge chunk of her future lay at the end of this highway.

The sky became both beautiful and powerful as lightning slashed and scarred. It seemed to hold, then grow and shudder, sending out endless fingers of fire. Although she'd told herself to be ready for the next cannon shot, when it came, she barely stifled a squeak. The car shuddered. She would swear it briefly lost contact with the road. She wanted to pull over and wait out the anger and energy, but if she did, she'd have to park near the encroaching Everglades. For reasons she didn't want to examine, that frightened her more than driving through lightning and thunder and punishing downpour.

Frightened...or something else?

Creatures that should have never been spawned dwelled in the Everglades. Alligators, panthers, snakes—massive, slithering, silent snakes. That's what upset her, not the sense that she was about to be challenged, changed.

Once again lightning rent the sky. The incredible display called her to it.

Now going little more than twenty miles an hour, she headed arrow-like toward the blue and black horizon. A moment ago she'd been terrified. Terror now turned into fascination. This monster of energy and might held her in its grip. She gave herself up to it as she'd long dreamed of giving herself, totally and without will or thought, to a man and became nothing except nerves and sight and hearing.

In that secret dream she walked naked and hot with need toward a dark, faceless man. His powerful body hummed, challenged, promised. Urged by his silent command, she'd dropped to her knees before his spread legs and lowered her head in submission. Waiting for him to claim her.

When he gripped her hair and forced her to look up at him, her body heated even more. Became less hers. She immediately arched her back and offered him her breasts which he took in his large, rough hands. The work-hardened paws claimed her breasts, flattening her swollen nipples against his palms. He began a demanding, slow circular motion that brought her to a place somewhere between pain and climax. Her clit swelled and became wet, and with breath and eyes, she begged him to thrust his cock into her. To end the wanting. He wore only tight black briefs, and his hard penis filled them. But she knew not to touch him until he gave her permission.

But then...then...

Movement on her left pulled Mala back from the brink of madness and ecstasy, burying but not killing the fantasy and her unchecked reaction. She was being passed, not by a car, but a death-black motorcycle. Its rider crouched low over the beast like an Indian riding a wild stallion—or a man riding a woman. Maybe her. He wore a helmet so dark it was nearly impossible to determine where it left off and the thunder-born landscape began. If it hadn't been for the clear face mask, she might not know whether a man or woman was on board.

A man.

He passed slowly, not cautiously so much as if he was determined to get an intimate look at her and didn't care how long it took, or whether exceeding her speed put him in jeopardy. She tried to take her eyes off him, but the man held her with something, maybe nothing more than an extension of the forces which existed around and above and beyond them.

She took in his bulk, the power and size and agility of him, and wondered if any woman had ever tamed the wildness she sensed in him. If she might be that woman. The motorcycle, lean and sleek and dangerous, seemed hard-put to battle wind and rain. A lesser man would have been forced to stop, or been blown off the road before he could.

Not this panther-man.

Her gaze didn't waver from him until he'd passed. Nothing else mattered during those seconds when their eyes met and locked and communicated something which now rode deep and hot in her belly.

It couldn't be. She wasn't feeling sexual excitement! *Yeah, right.*

He was a stranger, a damn fool risking his life on an all-but-deserted highway in danger of being overtaken by the ravenous jungle. He couldn't possibly sense that he embodied her secret and unattainable fantasy.

He was arrogant and self-confident, a physical creature who leaped from one adventure to another, one sexual partner after another, seeking release for his boundless energy. Whether there really were such men, or whether they simply existed deep and untapped and usually unacknowledged in her subconscious, she didn't know, didn't care.

He was man. Animal. Sex. Storm and darkness, woven seamlessly into the environment.

Now he was ahead of her. He'd eased up a little as if he'd sensed her speed and easily matched his to hers the way her dream master-lover knew how to bring her to the brink of climax again and again—to extend the awful, sweet torture. She could tell he was a large man, well over six feet, with shoulders so wide that if she tried to wrap her arms around them, she'd be hard pressed to do so. A man like that could never be controlled. He was a master of control.

Get a grip, right now!

He wore nothing to protect himself from the liquid spear points slamming into him. The lack of a coat didn't surprise her. Even in the midst of a storm, the temperature seldom dropped below eighty degrees. Still, his bare hands and arms and throat must be taking a terrible beating. It occurred to her that her vehicle would provide him with protection and wondered why he'd passed instead of remaining behind her.

He looked over his shoulder. Again those eyes, all but hidden under their Plexiglas protection, reached for her, grabbed hold of the hungry woman in her and said something silent, and elemental, and undeniable.

She took in several open-mouthed breaths and tried to force her attention on what had brought her out here today, but the case filled with silver and abalone jewelry which rode on the seat beside her no longer mattered. Only this rain slickened highway, the dark unknown on either side did. The panther-man ahead of her.

Mostly the man.

She was now going just under twenty miles an hour, her speed determined by the motorcyclist. He must have realized he'd made a mistake by passing and wanted back the scant rain-break her car provided. After several minutes of indecision, she pulled into the passing lane. Keeping far to the left to reduce the amount of water her tires threw at him, she touched the gas pedal.

He was looking at her again, those shadowed eyes sealing them together. Something that tasted too much like fear invaded her. She absorbed it until it changed into need which found a home at the joining of her legs. The heat she now felt had nothing to do with outside temperatures and everything to do with desire and fantasy.

Fantasy.

The rain would cease. He'd stop his motorcycle. She'd pull over next to him and get out. He'd dismount, take off his helmet, revealing ebony hair and eyes which carried the same compelling color and spear her with his gaze. He'd reach out his hand, not in question, but command. She'd place hers in it, warm and strong and wet, leather against silk. With him leading the way, they'd step into the jungle. The jungle would absorb them.

"Strip," he'd say. "Now."

And she would. The civilized woman whose days were filled with trying to earn a living would cease to exist. Instead, she'd allow herself the heady freedom of focusing totally on her body and on his. To hell with responsibility. Her heart would beat like a drum in a hard-rock band. She'd stare at his totally naked body, not a quick and furtive glance, but bold and open because he belonged to her—just as she belonged to him. It would be night, endless night and endless sex.

That's enough! Get a grip!

She was ahead of him. Feeling less in control than she imagined possible, she concentrated on the complex task of herding her car back to the right. After a moment, she again saw him in her rear view mirror. The storm showed no sign of exhausting itself, and she told herself that the least she could do was run interference for this reckless rider. He'd be grateful for her thoughtfulness. He'd—

This wasn't a man ruled by gratitude. Not gentle. Confident of his power over women.

How she'd come to that conclusion didn't matter. This was her fantasy. Hadn't her creativity always been ignited by the colors and sounds and messages of nature?

Only today, a man who was both stallion and panther, not nature, held her. She tried to imagine him in suit and tie responding to voice mail and faxes, hunched over a computer, corporate decisions an everyday occurrence.

No. This was a physical man. What she'd seen of his shoulders and back and arms and legs told her that. He earned his living with the strength in that work-honed body.

The possibility that he shared his world with a woman nearly made her scream. Hands locked around the steering wheel, she entertained the image of ripping out that woman's throat. Reminding herself that he wasn't hers to claim, she tried to imagine where he lived, whether he walked into an empty house at the end of the day or—why should she feel this way about a man she didn't know?

Not a house. A boat.

Where that thought came from she couldn't say, but it fit with what her imagination was creating. He'd fall asleep lulled by waves and the sound of seabirds. He knew and loved and accepted the rhythm of the ocean. Maybe he was the descendant of pirates.

A pirate took what he wanted. Armed with knives and confidence, he'd seize a woman and throw her, bound and helpless, onto his boat. He'd stand over her, legs widespread to reveal the awesome size of his penis. Fear would weaken his captive's limbs and when he knelt and straddled her, she'd beg for mercy.

Mercy? He didn't know the meaning of the word.

Mala was telling herself she'd taken the fantasy over the edge when she realized she couldn't see him. She panicked, terrified he'd hit something or been knocked off balance by a powerful gust of wind and was being slammed to the pavement.

When he emerged from her blind spot and began to pull alongside again, relief washed through her. That and an appetite for what he was which clawed and demanded. She looked over at him, nodding casually in the hope he wouldn't suspect what was taking place inside her. He didn't return her lying nod, and it seemed as if his gaze was a little less remote and disturbing. More knowing.

The rain served as a filmy curtain between them. When lightning burst, she was momentarily blinded. Blinking, she now perceived him as an outline, still strong and competent, too dark. He and the motorcycle had become one. The pavement beneath and wilderness behind and beyond all blended into a nearly indefinable whole.

Crack! Crack!

The twin thunderclaps reminded her of how wrong she was to think she could exert any control over the weather. She waited with a concentration that separated her from the reality of the man she shared the road with. When she looked for him again he was—

Sliding. Motorcycle out of control! Too-thin tires fighting to grip slickened pavement. Plowing into the Everglades.

"No!"

Chapter Two

Mala slammed on her brakes. The car jerked to the left and away from what she could still see of the rapidly disappearing motorcycle, but she fought until her vehicle once again obeyed her command. Although some portions of the country between Naples and Fort Lauderdale were little more than swampy prairie, along here the Everglades were everything tourists and residents alike expected of one of the few truly wild areas left. Great moss-hung cypress, saw palmetto stands, pools of dark swamp water, endless muck, all that and more waited for the out-of-control motorcycle and its hard-muscled, helpless rider.

What had happened didn't matter. Neither did why. Metal and rubber and flesh and bone were being sucked into the wilderness, not by accident, but because some force dwelled in that vastness of water and vegetation. Whoever, *whatever* it was had snared her fantasy man and was bent on claiming it.

"No!"

Although everything remained a blur coated by the raging sky, she knew he was gripping the handlebars with every ounce of strength in his body. His foot massaged the brakes as he sought that delicate balance between a hard slam and a controlled slowing. If the pavement hadn't been greased with water, his expert handling would have won the battle, but nature had lined up with the opposition. Nothing he did or might do was enough.

She watched him slide almost gracefully out of view, dense foliage and more swallowing him. Although her own squealing brakes and the blood pounding in her temples made a disturbing jumble of sound, she half believed she heard him yell in defiance and denial.

Then he was gone.

"No!" she screamed again. Even before her car stopped rocking, she'd killed the motor and hurtled herself out into the deluge. She was instantly soaked, rain running off her hair and chin and arms. Her sandals were meant for carrying her through a humid day of peddling her wares, not entering the Everglades. Even if they were, could she bring herself to put civilization behind her?

Trapped by indecision, she danced on her toes on the graveled shoulder and stared at where she'd last seen the motorcycle and its rider. Although she weighed just 120 pounds, she was already sinking into the rain-saturated sand. How much worse it must be for the man if he'd landed in swampy ground.

Of course he had. She had no doubt that his forward movement would take him into this living, breathing wilderness.

Shaken, she took a few more cautious steps. She tried to walk beyond what a highway crew had deposited in an all-but-futile effort at providing a barrier between road and jungle, but the sodden ground gripped her shoe, and she jerked back.

"Can you hear me? Please, can you hear me?"

Nothing.

"Where are you? I'll—I've got to get help. Please! Answer me. Please!"

Silence.

No, not really silence. The rain, wind, and thunder, even the erratic lightning created a noise that was more essence than sound. Woven into that was the music of the Everglades, a constant deep hum. She knew this highway, understood a little about how hard it had been to wrestle a thin, firm strip from the wilderness, but she'd never imagined herself walking into that wasteland.

Until today.

"Can you hear me? Please! Are you all right?"

Darkness. The stench of things wet and rotting. A humming which seemed to grow and expand until his body felt as if it might explode. Mosquitoes which drove him half mad with their insistence. He lay on his side in a bog, his right leg burned from where it had struck the motorcycle's exhaust pipe, and his mind searching, questioning. The cycle was gone now, maybe a victim of quicksand. Laird Jaeger fought back the icy taste and touch of something he refused to claim, but the effort left him without the strength for anything else. He was alive! Lost. Scared.

No, damn it, not afraid! He became aware of liquid seeping around him, but whatever he'd landed in, it wasn't about to suck him down to where he couldn't breathe or see.

Knowing he didn't immediately have to fight the swamp allowed him to gain a small measure of control. Warning himself not to panic, he took in his situation.

He'd been riding his motorcycle through Alligator Alley. It had been raining, the deluge accompanied by a display of light and sound that had filled him with reckless abandon, an emotion he knew as well as he did the restlessness that was part of his nature. The percussion which accompanied the thunder had actually lifted him off the ground, and he'd been hard pressed to see the divider strip, but then nature had always exerted her control over him. He'd never thought to fight it.

Drawing in a deep and steadying breath, he identified the smell as swamp gases. Bottom line was that his mode of transportation was gone. He had no idea how far he was from the road or what direction he needed to head in order to find it. At least nothing felt broken. It was still raining, a curtain of water only partially deflected by the trees that draped themselves over and around and beyond him.

Trees. Dense and lush. Full of life. Nothing to need to escape. Nothing dangerous.

Encouraged by that bit of logic, he pushed through the fog in his mind. There'd been a woman on the highway with him. She had long hair, straight and dark and soft around her angled features. Big eyes that found and locked with his. He'd read unfulfilled sexual need in those eyes and had taken advantage of it. With nothing more than the energy that had been part of him since becoming a man, he'd spoken to her need. She'd responded. If things hadn't changed, he would have bedded her. It was as simple as that.

Where was she?

Where was he?

The question brought with it a spasm of emotion. The sounds were of the jungle, without beginning or end, beyond his comprehension and yet—

"Thunder."

Shaken by something that felt as if it existed inside him, he forced himself into a sitting position. A sharp sting along his right palm alerted him to the fact that he'd cut himself. The injury might have happened while he was being catapulted into the swamp, but perhaps the saw grass was responsible, not that it mattered.

"*Thunder.*"

"What?" He forced the word. "Is there someone here?"

Even as the impenetrable foliage absorbed his question, he regretted speaking. He hadn't heard anyone call out. The sound was nothing more than system overload. He glared at a ten-foot-high wall of greenery. He'd always felt imprisoned by enclosures, and if he didn't keep up his guard, that emotion might rule him now. He became aware of just how spongy the ground under him was. Although he was the furthest thing from being squeamish, he didn't want to go on sitting. His legs felt less dependable than he needed them to be, his head both light and heavy.

There was no way out.

Moving deliberately, he looked around slowly. Began wrestling understanding from insanity.

He had to have made some kind of an impression on the jungle-growth, tire tracks, grasses flattened, something, but he couldn't determine where he'd come from, or where his motorcycle had gone. His helmet had been torn from him. What drew his hand to his back pocket where he kept his wallet, he couldn't say. He didn't encounter the familiar lump.

No identification. No mode of transportation. Minus the head protection he'd strapped himself into.

"*Thunder.*"

He breathed through his mouth to lessen the impact of the swamp's stench and fight a touch of panic, then gave himself the task, not of determining where the "sound" had come from, but of finding his way out. He couldn't have gone very far. Shouldn't he hear highway sounds, glimpse open space beyond the living fence that held him prisoner? He wanted to be back on his motorcycle and changing leads with the woman.

Something warm and wet slid between his toes. He wore no boots. Like the helmet and wallet, they'd been stolen from him.

A wistful whisper distracted him from unanswerable questions. It seemed to be human.

The woman in the car? The one he'd known would spread her legs and beg him to spear her.

"Where are you?" he bellowed. The cry had nothing to do with the need for sex and everything to do with survival.

"Thunder."

Steeling himself against the whisper, he commanded himself to focus on the woman who represented a sane and orderly world. He'd long had a certain power over the female sex—animal magnetism his brother had called it—but until now he'd only used that indefinable something to get them into his bed. Now mentally reaching her might save his life. He had no choice but to try.

"I'm here. Waiting for you. You can't fight it. Don't even try."

Barely daring to breathe, he waited a moment. He had no idea whether his thoughts had reached her, but if they had, he needed to give her more.

"Become animal—an animal in need.

"Find me. Let me satisfy that need.

"Find me!"

Trying to project his thoughts over God knew how many miles exhausted him. Either she heard his plea and command or she didn't. Right now he had to make order out of insanity.

Somehow.

Mala held her breath and willed what had caught her attention to repeat itself, but it didn't. She was forced to admit she must have imagined she'd heard a human voice. She could wait for him to reappear, at which time she'd offer him the shelter of her car and maybe a hell of a lot more. What made more sense was to go after help. That option would hold more water—an unfunny cliché given the weather and circumstances—if she hadn't been halfway between two very distant points of civilization. The final alternative was to take courage in hand and plunge in after a man who might be injured and at the mercy of both the elements and his injuries.

Hurt? She hated the thought, and yet if he was, she could minister to him. She again tried to leave the manmade footing. As before, she immediately bogged down. Even if she managed to make her way into the growth, she couldn't cover more than a few hard-won inches at a time. As she extracted her sandal from the muck, another unsettling thought occurred to her. The motorcycle's forward motion had taken the man into the jungle, but he wouldn't have gone very far before the jungle stopped the machine. Still, she couldn't see or hear him. If she took off after him, how long would it take for her to become lost?

She didn't want to think about that happening to the man, but the image of him wandering aimlessly among endless trees and moss and swamps and grasses with the rain a waterfall took hold. Was it possible for a person to become so disoriented within a stone's throw of a highway that he'd never find his way out?

Of course not!

Probably not.

"Can you hear me? Answer me! Damn it, answer me!"

Nothing.

It wasn't until she'd traveled close to twenty miles that Mala spotted a highway patrol vehicle pulling away from a viewpoint. By then, the rain had slackened enough that her wipers were equal to their task. As she jumped out of her car, she gave a quick thought to how bedraggled she must look, but it didn't matter. Only rescuing the man who'd turned her world and body on end did.

"Where did you say he left the road?" the too-young officer asked in response to her garbled explanation. "Can you take me there?"

She nodded. She wondered if he'd tell her to lead the way and asked herself if she could concentrate on driving well enough to pull it off. Fortunately, after telling his dispatcher or sergeant or whoever he was talking to what had happened, he indicated he wanted her to sit beside him in his vehicle.

Although she was relieved to have found someone who'd know what to do, she swore he was barely going fast enough to justify having started the engine. She wanted to pound her fist against him and scream at him to hurry. Realizing she'd started shivering, she tried to determine whether he'd turned on the air conditioning, but her eyes refused to focus. Maybe the truth was that she couldn't take her attention off what lurked at the edge of the highway long enough to concentrate on anything else.

More likely the truth was that she still felt sexually stimulated.

A man was out in that tangled vastness. Alone. Lost. Dependent on her when, damn it, she had no idea what to do.

"There." She pointed. "I hope—oh no. He's not... He's still in there, isn't he?"

The patrolman—he'd said his name was Todd something—pulled over to the side of the road. She was out of the car before he'd unstrapped his seat belt. Belatedly, she remembered to look down to where the motorcycle tire tracks should be. The sky had lost its deep plum hue, and the sun was regaining control, but despite the improved conditions, she saw nothing, heard nothing except what lived and breathed deep in the wilderness. She fought the stupid impulse to yank off her clothes and plunge into that wilderness.

"You're sure this is where it happened?" Todd asked.

"I'm sure," she said, irritated. Her nerve endings, the tips of her fingers and base of her throat and pit of her stomach told her that this was the spot where she'd stood not so long ago.

She had to give Todd and the highway department their due. Todd called for backup, and two other patrol vehicles soon arrived. All told, five uniformed officers scoured the side of the highway for a half mile in either direction. When they wandered afield of where he'd disappeared, she couldn't blame them. After all, the ground bore no signs to indicate a man on an out-of-control piece of machinery had been here.

Still, she was so sure that when Todd pointed out that, given the lack of evidence, they'd concluded there'd been no accident, she practically had to be dragged away. She climbed into the patrol car, but kept her eyes fixed on where he'd disappeared until she could no longer see the forlorn spot.

When Todd deposited her back at her vehicle, he assured her a tracking dog would be brought in for one final search. Then he suggested that because of the heavy downpour, she might have imagined what she'd seen. She nearly yelled at him that a man's life was at stake here, but he and four other trained men had spent two hours trying to find some sign of her elusive rider.

After giving Todd her home phone number, she got into her car, but instead of heading toward Fort Lauderdale where she was expected, she pulled a U-turn.

"I know I saw you. You're real! Damn it, I know you exist."

A large truck and trailer barreled past, the blast of air swirling her limp hair about her face. Mala grabbed the dark length with one hand and held it against the nape of her neck. Fighting a deep sense of failure, she tried to reassure herself that someone would report the man as missing, and she'd be vindicated. But the only thing that mattered was that a man—strong and young with a lifetime ahead of him—was out there somewhere.

Trapped.

Trapped? She recoiled from the thought, but couldn't argue it away. Logic said he must be injured or dead. Otherwise, why hadn't he stumbled out?

However, something she couldn't put a name to told her that neither of those things was true. Like a caged animal, she paced the narrow shoulder. The sun had returned, but it had done nothing to make her footing less treacherous. If that dog didn't find anything, no further search would be made. Her man would remain lost.

Her man?

No. Hardly that.

More like the other way around.

"What do you want me to do?"

Stay.

Whimpering, Mala backed away until she collided with her car. She couldn't have heard anything! She couldn't!

And yet—

"Are you there? Why don't you show yourself?"

I can't.

She was losing her mind. "Why not? This—this is—why not?"

I don't know.

"Don't—know?" She tried to go on, but her throat dried up. There were more vehicles on the highway now. The people in those cars and trucks might be taking note of the crazy lady standing dangerously close to the wilderness, talking to it, pacing. Her body on fire.

"What's your name?" *Please fuck me! Please!* "Who are you?"

Laird Jaeger.

His throat was dry, but he didn't dare dip his hands into the stagnant pond. He'd been on the move for hours. His jeans were ruined, his feet raw. When the heat and humidity had become too much, he'd taken off his shirt. He swore he'd tied it around his waist, but it was gone now, lost in the nothingness that had claimed him. His pockets were empty, his mind void of everything except the need for survival.

That and the connection he'd made with the woman.

She was gone now, and although he understood she wouldn't wait forever for his return, he was angry that she had so little faith in him. Yet why should he expect anything else? He'd had hours in which to make sense of what had happened and get back to the world he knew, but he hadn't been able to accomplish that pig-simple task.

Instead, there'd been endless bugs and frogs, grass-choked swamp, dark pools and barely moving canals. Had he been going in circles, traveling deeper and deeper into nothing?

Panting against the heat, he waited for fear to envelop him, but it still didn't. It was almost as if he belonged here. As if he accepted he would die here.

What made him think that? Dying wasn't even on his radar, and how could he think he belonged someplace when he didn't know where it was?

He heard a limpkin's wailing cry. A distant alligator bellowed. The call seemed right, proud and defiant. When the roaring, buzzing, hissing, screaming noises circled him, he kept himself from becoming lost in the music by concentrating on another sound—a woman's cry. He "spoke" to her, again told her his name, demanded she not forget him.

Hour upon hour, he sensed nothing except harsh, ancient smells and that unholy din, thirst and hunger and the unending question of why he'd been brought here. Someone, or something, had taken hold of him, stripped him of who and what he'd always been, thrust him into this uncivilized place. Was here with him.

"I will not go through this alone," he told the woman. "*You will come to me. You will.*"

Chapter Three

The air conditioning wasn't working in the Fort Lauderdale motel room, but Mala was barely aware of the sticky heat. After placing the case containing her jewelry on the small table, she kicked off her sandals and collapsed on the bed.

She lay staring at the speckled ceiling, her thoughts going places her tired body couldn't. She'd spent what was left of daylight prowling Alligator Alley. Hugging the side of the road had done nothing to sway her conviction that she had been right about where she'd directed Todd and his fellow patrolmen to look.

Not that being sure had changed anything, she admitted as she became aware of the blinking telephone light. Because she'd told Sandy where she'd be staying, it had to be her friend trying to get in touch with her. The past five years had been a journey to where she was tonight career-wise, and yet it no longer mattered because a stranger on a motorcycle had become more important. Had penetrated her in frightening, exciting ways.

Still—

On the tail of a sigh, she sat up and dialed the motel operator who informed her that Sandy had left three messages asking—insisting—she get in touch with her immediately.

"Where the hell have you been?" Sandy demanded before

Mala had time to do more than say hello.

"It's a long story. I'm sorry. I know you were worried."

"Yeah, I was, old kid. But that isn't the half of it. Ralph called asking if the three of us could get together for dinner tonight instead of waiting to meet in his office tomorrow. Naturally I said yes, and then when I couldn't get hold of you, I had to cancel. I don't know what he's going to think. Hopefully chalk it up to artistic temperament. I just hope he won't decide you're undependable."

Ralph Korn of Southeast Jewelry Unlimited had long dealt with independent crafts people. He wouldn't be successful if he hadn't developed an instinct about those who could be depended on. Sandy would have done her best to make things right, but they deserved an explanation. The apology she could handle. As for the explanation—

"Where were you?" Sandy demanded.

"What?" she asked, then struggled to correct herself. "You don't have time for the whole story. Besides, if I get going, I'll sound like an idiot." *Or sex-starved, which I am.* "I'll try to make sense of it in the morning. The meeting's still set for then, right?"

"Yes. You're not going to blow it. You've worked too damn hard, and you're incredibly talented. You deserve this break. All right. Enough of the morale booster and lecture. I'm serious, though. The competition's intense. I'm thinking we need to get together before early tomorrow. What if..."

Mala tuned her friend out, paying just enough attention that if Sandy asked another question, hopefully she'd be able to field it, but knowing Sandy, it would be a long time before she ran down. Her friend was right. Tomorrow could be a major turning point in her life, and she should be wired. She had been until the storm and the man.

Laird Jaeger.

What had it been, mind control? More like body control along with something that stirred her as she'd never been before.

Still holding on to the receiver, she turned on the lamp, then reached for her case and opened it. Light spilled over compartments filled with necklaces, bracelets, and earrings, all created from her trademark abalone and silver. She'd been making jewelry inspired by sunsets and sunrises, dew on leaves, pristine beaches and white-flecked waves since she was in high school, experimenting and refining until these pieces and hundreds of others like them became an extension of herself. Now, in part because of Sandy's connections, she had the opportunity to become a full-time jewelry maker.

"Sandy," she said finally. "I'll be there. I promise."

After hanging up, she stared at the samples of her work Ralph Korn would be looking at tomorrow, but then her vision blurred, and she lay back down on the thin coverlet. Sandy had called her dependable, but she wasn't. Otherwise, she wouldn't have left Laird Jaeger alone.

Laird Jaeger.

She felt, not exactly a presence, but *something* settle beside her. Whatever it was felt like pinpricks along the length of her backbone, heightened awareness at the base of her spine most of all, growing warmth in her pelvic region. With her eyes resolutely closed, she surrendered to whatever it was.

"You're mine. You have to be."

"Why?" she whispered.

"Whatever is happening, I will not go through it alone."

"What can I do? I failed to—"

"This was meant to be."

"The accident?"

"No accident. Fate."

Fate. The warmth in her belly and beyond increased, demanded attention. Moaning, she turned onto her side and pressed her hand hard against her stomach. Already her breasts felt too swollen for her bra.

"I'm doing what I have to. You're my connection to the world. I must have that. Must keep you with me."

Although she didn't move, barely breathed, Mala felt a man's hand cover hers, pull it off her belly and replace it with his own. Shivering, she asked herself the vital, stupid question: did she want this? Hell yes!

Impatient with clothing, he yanked off her shorts as if he had every right to do whatever he wanted with and to her and threw them on the floor. Her practical briefs no longer hugged her waist, but had been pulled half off her hips. She waited for them to join her shorts. Instead, a hand that felt like fine sandpaper slid under the fabric. In her mind—maybe only in her mind—she spread her legs. She felt so damn exposed, like a mare in heat waiting to be mounted.

Strong, short fingernails teased away her pubic hair and found willing flesh. His other hand settled over her hipbone and pressed her against the mattress. She arched her spine, but although she might have been able to break free, that was the last thing on her mind. In truth she wasn't sure she still had a brain, not that it mattered. Forget self-restraint. Bring on an old-fashioned dose of sex. For an excruciating length of time, he simply held her prisoner while his nails tasted and tested the rounded bulge in front of her clit. She couldn't think past the exploration. Wanted more.

He knew what he was doing. Oh damn, did he.

"Don't...make me..." *Don't make me wait, please,* she

finished silently.

She heard laughter. A moment later the hand slid fully between her legs. He cupped her cunt and pressed. For maybe a half-second she was terrified of his bold possession, but what the hell. He wasn't here in the flesh. Besides, whatever was going on was a thousand times better than masturbating.

Sometimes raking lightly, sometimes pressing with enough force that it bordered on the painful, he branded her now pulsating bud. He teased at the entrance to her passage as she broke out in a sweat, but although he must know how desperately she wanted it, he didn't penetrate. Just the same, she felt herself rising, rising, growing and becoming hot. No, not just hot. On fire! It was happening so fast. So hard. So close to climax. So close!

"Fuck me," she begged. "Damn you, do it!"

"No."

"Damn you."

"Not yet."

"Yet? What—" Before she could continue, he caught her swollen bud between thumb and forefinger. Gasping, she arched toward him, nearly levitating off the bed. Just one more touch, please, just one and she'd be there. Gone!

"No! Please," she gasped when suddenly, cruelly, he released her. "Don't stop. Not now!"

"Soon. I promise."

Still on fire, she threw herself into a sitting position and looked wildly around. She was wet between her legs. Throbbed. On the brink.

Brought to that place by a man who existed only in her mind. Who spoke and commanded and claimed in ways that defied description and both thrilled and terrified her. Like a drunk without a drink for too long, she couldn't focus on anything except the next time. And there would be a next, damn it! Only, when he again clamped his hard, powerful hand over her cunt, he'd better be there in person.

There was a glow like hundreds of fireflies, except they formed a human outline.

More curious than afraid, Laird watched the approaching pinpricks of light. Not long ago he'd been determined to put the pieces of this crazy puzzle that had become his life together, but something, maybe the vegetation, had blunted the edges of his determination. He'd never call himself passive, but there was nothing wrong with accepting the status quo. Being more interested in what lay ahead of him than what he'd given up. He wanted to stand, but his muscles refused to obey his command. Although he knew he'd find nothing, he reached for the front jeans pocket which always held a small knife, but even if he still had it, what good was a short blade against fireflies?

"Thunder."

For a half beat, the jungle silenced, leaving only the single, haunting word. It seemed to have come from the glowing outline, but he couldn't be sure. The figure—did he dare call it that?—glided closer. If there was a face, the night kept it hidden from him. He saw long, lean limbs, wispy and yet real. The man, or whatever it was, didn't appear to be wearing anything. If he had such things as feet, they didn't seem to be touching the ground.

A shadow, a shade, a shape unlike anything he'd ever seen. Because his eyes weren't telling him enough, Laird tried to smell whatever now hovered less than ten feet away, but the swamp-stench was too strong. Either that or this ghostly creature smelled exactly like his surroundings.

"Who are you?" he demanded.

"Night Hunter."

Laird jerked back. At the same time, the "thing" called to him in a way more powerful than any woman ever had. Crouching, he waited out a distant panther's scream. "What are you, Night Hunter? What—"

"Listen and learn, Thunder."

Was this creature who wanted to be known as Night Hunter calling him Thunder? Before he could decide whether to ask, the big cat again filled the air with its primal cry. There *was* the remotest possibility that a panther lived this close to civilization, but in his heart of hearts, he knew that wasn't the case.

"Is that what you want me to hear?" he asked. "The panther?"

"He rules this land. Has since the first People came here."

"Not anymore." Why was he arguing? "Thanks to man, his existence is in danger."

"You are wrong."

Something beyond his comprehension was happening all right. His thigh muscles burned from the effort of remaining at the ready, but he didn't dare relax his guard. Now, when he was exhausted and it was too dark to risk walking on ground that might shred his feet, he felt a powerful need to follow Night Hunter.

But where? Why?

"What do you mean, wrong?" he finally thought to ask.

"Soon." Night Hunter's voice became a seductive whisper luring him from the woman he'd been trying to reach since losing control of his motorcycle and world. "Soon you will understand. And take your rightful place with your people."

"My place? What..."

Night Hunter shimmered. It was as if his body, or what passed for his body, had begun to dance with the wind. "As chief of the Seminole."

Gasping for breath, Mala shot upright. After what she'd been through today, she couldn't believe she'd dozed off. She now felt as if she was sharing her body and mind with someone else. Thank heavens the lamp was still on because if it hadn't been, she wasn't sure she'd remember who and what she was. She concentrated on making herself as receptive as possible to whatever message Laird Jaeger might be trying to send, but nothing reached her.

Nothing. The word was a mockery of everything she'd done and tried to do today. Everything he'd done to her.

Sliding her legs off the bed, she started to stand when something occurred to her. Feeling like a fool for not having thought of it before, she reached for the Fort Lauderdale phone book. A study of the directory revealed no Laird Jaeger or anyone remotely resembling that name. Undaunted, she dialed information and asked if there were any Jaegers listed in Naples. There were three, including a fishing boat rental place called Jaeger Boats. Armed with the two residential numbers in addition to the boat business, she started making calls. To her growing alarm, no one answered.

"Are they out looking for you?" she asked. Caught in the image of a frantic family, she prowled to the window and looked down at a well-lighted swimming pool filled with children despite the late hour. The normal sounds should soothe her and keep her rooted in the real world, but she couldn't concentrate on anything beyond what Laird Jaeger must be going through, if he wasn't dead.

He wasn't. She was certain of that.

"I'm here." Her voice was the barest whisper. "Waiting for you. Whatever you want or need, I'll give it to you." She parted her lips and sucked two fingers into her warm, moist opening. The thought of what could happen when they met in the flesh sent a streak of electricity through her.

He was alone again because Night Hunter had been absorbed by the jungle. Laird listened to primal sounds brought into awful clarity because there was nothing else to concentrate on. Night Hunter existed. What or who he was, Laird couldn't say, but he'd been visited by something with intelligence that had sought him out for purposes not yet revealed.

His feet were less tender than they'd been when he began his barefoot journey. He had no doubt that if he remained out here much longer, he could fashion a weapon out of wood and vine and other materials and bring down the game he needed to stay alive. He'd reach deep inside himself to that place where the skills of his ancestors remained for that.

Ancestors? He wasn't Indian.

Something was climbing over his instep. He flicked it away and went about gathering the leaves and other softened things he'd need for sleeping. Once he'd layered the ground with his find, he stretched out and stared until he found a thin tunnel to the sky not obscured by trees.

There were a few stars about, distant and cold, yet comforting. He wondered if that cat or one of its relatives would sense the helpless human being come after an easy meal, but he had no more apprehension about a panther than he did about living on a boat even when he anchored far from land.

He was safe here because Night Hunter had so willed it. And because a part of him he'd just begun to fathom had long waited for this night.

Suddenly restless, he flattened a hand over his chest. He was aware, not just of the strong line of ribs beneath his flesh, but his heart tucked safely within its shelter. He'd heard the word lonely analyzed and struggled against by everyone he'd come in contact with, but the emotion had always seemed abstract and unimportant to him.

Now, alone in a place that perceived humans as unwelcome intruders, he should be cowering. But what he felt wasn't isolation and abject solitude so much as a longing for something never before realized. That and power that went beyond muscle and bone.

It was easy to remember what she looked like. It had started as a game, a stupid man ignoring the downpour because he'd glimpsed a beautiful young woman driving alone. But after the first time he looked into her eyes, it had stopped being a game. Wanting more than those too-big eyes and the dark waterfall of hair, he'd allowed her to pass and then overtaken her again.

He'd sensed her futile search for him on the tail of the vast energy it had taken to send her a message. He'd never believed in fate, psychic connection, or whatever they called it, but something had happened between them today that might have to last for as long as he survived in this harsh and honest place.

"Don't ignore me. Don't even try."

In his mind's eye, he saw her standing alone in a darkened room. She had several fingers in her mouth and was running her tongue over them, a look of sexual excitement in her half-closed eyes. Her other hand rested between her legs, a forefinger reaching deep inside her. Moaning, she jerked her hips back and forth.

"That will do, for now," he told her. "But when I take you, you will scream. Dance on my cock. Maybe, someday you will understand why I must do this."

Four in the morning, a time of quiet and rest, of recharging oneself for what the day might bring. Instead of trying to reclaim sleep, Mala sat in the unfamiliar bed. Leaning forward, she wrapped her arms around her bare knees and rocked gently.

Eyes closed, she mentally skimmed over lush foliage until she half believed she could see what rested at the base of the palmettos. She smiled at images of raccoons, deer, turtles, bright green frogs and exquisitely beautiful birds, but those creatures commanded only a small corner of her mind. Laird Jaeger was out there somewhere.

As thoughts of alligators and panthers and snakes replaced those of gentle deer and white-feathered birds, she scrambled out of bed. Her nightgown was supposed to be knee-length, but she must have thrashed about so that it was now wound about her waist. Either that or her phantom not-quite-lover was responsible.

Determined not to let carnal need control her again, she yanked on jogging shorts and tucked her nightgown into the waistband. Then she grabbed her purse and stepped into the empty hall. She didn't encounter anyone in the parking lot, a good thing because how could she explain what she was doing?

I lost a man earlier today. And now I'm going out on a moonless night to see if I can find him.

Right!

After starting her car, she headed west. By the time she reached Alligator Alley, the first hint of day had begun. No matter how hard she fought, she couldn't deny or ignore the need humming between her legs. She turned on her radio and flipped through stations, but there was no news of a missing man.

"I'm coming, I'm coming," she muttered, the hollow promise in time with the sound her tires made. A few people were already on the road. None had any hint that something terrifying and unexplainable had happened out here yesterday.

It still wasn't light enough that she could get by without headlights by the time she pulled off the road, and she could only pray Laird had survived his pitch-black night. She killed the engine, but instead of getting out, she leaned forward against the steering wheel. If only she could kill, or at least ignore, the weight of unfilled sexual need.

Stop feeling as if she was in heat.

Through the open window, she caught smells and sounds that must have taken over Laird's every thought. While she was driving, she'd half convinced herself she'd find him waiting for her. She'd invite him into her car. Eyes locked with hers, his strong hand gripping her arm, he'd tell her how he'd escaped and how he wouldn't have been able to do it if it hadn't been for her. How he intended to reward her.

She'd admit he'd found his way into her dreams, and she'd wakened early because she'd known the time to get him had arrived. They'd shake their heads and then—

And then he'd take her in his arms and explain he'd survived so he could have her. Then he'd strip off her clothes and...

He wasn't here.

Fear surged through her, and she pounded her fist against

the steering wheel. "This can't be happening! It can't!"

But it had. That reality propelled her out of the car. It wasn't until she was standing on warm, slithering sand that she realized she'd left the motel room without her shoes.

He didn't have any either. She knew that as clearly as she'd ever known anything.

"What happened to them?" she managed. A truck rumbled past, pushing hot air against her.

"I don't know."

Weak with relief, she sagged against her car's fender. "Are you all right?"

"Yes."

"What do you want me to do? I tried—the police didn't believe me. Why can't you come to me?"

"I don't know."

"Is there—"

"I'm not alone."

"You aren't?"

"Night Hunter."

"Who or what is that?"

"I don't know."

"Are you safe?"

"I think so."

"Thank God. I couldn't sleep," she babbled. "I kept thinking—I tried to call everyone in Naples with your name, but no one was home. Are they relatives?"

"Yes."

"What do you want me to do?"

"What's your name?"

"My—Mala Bey."

"Talk to me, Mala Bey."

Barely aware of what she was saying, she told him she was twenty-nine and lived near Naples, that she worked as a medical secretary but had been on her way to Fort Lauderdale because her best friend had shown her jewelry to a dealer and now, after years of working and learning and planning, she might finally be able to make a living doing what she most wanted. She left a great deal unsaid and yet told him what she wanted out of life, things that didn't matter to a man trapped in something neither of them understood.

"Are you married, Mala Bey?"

"No."

"Why not?"

"I came close. He was so damn considerate it drove me crazy. Always asking what I wanted. Trying to please."

"In bed?"

"Yes."

"I'm not that way."

"I know. You take."

"I do what I have to."

"Is that what it is? You get a kick out of—possessing me?"

"It's working, then?"

"I'm not going to answer that."

"It is. Good."

"All right!" she snapped. "You've gotten to me. Is that what you want to hear? I took two cold showers last night. I've never had to do that before in my life, but fat lot of good it did me. Before I'd even dried off—let me tell you something. If you could harvest and bottle up whatever the hell sexual stimulant you hit me with, you'd be rich. I'm not sure how I feel about it. Excited, if you must know, but also overwhelmed."

In the few minutes she'd been here, the sun had taken control of its domain. There was no end to the shades and hues of green. The artist in her made note of the subtle differences, but she hadn't come back here to store up impressions that found their way into her work.

She'd driven here barefoot because she'd had no choice. Because Laird Jaeger needed her.

Maybe as much as her turned-on body needed him.

Chapter Four

"You said something to me last night." Mala shook her head, trying to clear her thoughts. "About our—finding each other being fate."

Laird didn't answer, leaving her to ask if she'd really expected him to. While "talking" to him, she'd left the relative security of her car and walked to the edge of the Everglades. The vegetation's hold on her emotions felt almost as strong as Laird's hold did. Focused as she was on why she'd come here, she barely hesitated before pushing aside tall grass and branches and stepping into the rich-smelling growth. The Everglades' lushness infused her with strength. At the same time she feared it.

"What do you mean, fate?" she repeated. The skin at the back of her neck felt crawly and speaking came hard.

Only birds and insects responded. She heard highway sounds behind her, but this dense world, whether she was ready for it or not, had become her existence.

"You're making me crazy, you know." She tried a conversational tone. "If I had half the sense of a goat, I'd be on a shrink's couch right now. He'd take me through past lives, check for multiple personalities, make sure I hadn't been dropped on my head."

It wasn't her head that was—suddenly and unexpectedly—

making its presence known, but he didn't need to know that.

"I understand erotic fantasies," she continued. *More than I'm going to admit.* "But I'm—all right—I'll admit it, I'm used to controlling them, plugging in certain triggers such as a little leather and lace and indulging in some mental kinky fun, but knowing how to get in and out of the mood, playing it safe and in control, not the other way around."

"I told you. I had no choice."

"Is that what you said?" She squinted and stared. Had something changed about her surroundings? A darker-than-before hue to the area in front of that low-growing tree? She fought to concentrate. "I'm sorry. Of course you did."

She felt something feather-light on her cheek and brushed away what she hoped was a spider web. A not-too-subtle heat snaked through her groin and demanded a damn lot of attention. She pressed her thighs together and struggled to think about something, anything, except that sensation.

"When this is over, how about we both get on that shrink's couch," she blithered. "He could write a whole book on what we tell him, make his fortune and be awarded the Pulitzer or something."

Laird must not have thought she was funny because she didn't sense his response. Maybe she'd done a piss-poor job of hiding her arousal, and he was waiting to see what she'd do next.

"What?" she pressed. Lordy, it was hot and steamy back in here. "You think we should get our fifteen minutes of fame and to hell with him? Book ourselves onto talk shows, get on the cover of those tabloids?"

"What do you want out of life?"

"What?"

"I never asked myself that before. Wouldn't allow it."

Giving herself a mental shake that only partly deflected her focus on the area between her legs, she mulled over what he'd said. "You wouldn't allow it because you were too busy growing up, riding motorcycles, chasing women—not that you'd have to throw a net over them."

"Something like that."

If he hadn't sounded so reflective, she would have teased him. Or maybe she wouldn't. She'd been keeping a light tone because the whole insane scenario was easier to accept that way, but that approach wasn't getting her anywhere. Neither did it address his damnable mastery of her body.

"You're questioning the meaning of life now?" she asked.

"Something like—yeah."

"That's good, I think. Only, was it necessary for *this* to happen?" Unwilling to confess to what she meant by "this", she gnawed on her lower lip. Her surroundings hummed and hissed, and the warm, damp ground steamed. So did she.

No way about it, that one section over there was darker and denser than the rest of the leaves or whatever they called that stuff. She didn't want to stare, and yet she did.

After a few seconds, she could no longer call the object of her attention an anomaly or a reason to make an appointment with an optometrist. A shape was taking form—a man's shape.

Only, it wasn't a man. Not really. The size was right and what she concluded were shoulders were more than broad, thank you very much. A head, yes, a head. Except that he—she decided it was *him*—didn't have the traditional face. Instead, he was all eyes. Eyes with the power to hypnotize.

Energize.

Gentle and searching, maybe unsure or even lonely

beneath it all. No, she thought, I want you to be all-powerful, not human like the rest of us.

Forget the business with leather and lace. In her fantasy of fantasies, she imagined herself being thrown naked over a savage's shoulder and carted off to become his sex slave. Despite the erotic image, she didn't really want that, because she'd never been able to figure out what a sex slave did when her services weren't needed, except die of boredom.

"You're doing it again," she accused as her cunt whispered back to life. She wanted to explore and encourage the sensation, not fight it. "I'm here, all right! You got me to do what you wanted."

"Not entirely. Not yet."

But he was determined to change that. Wasn't the simmering, the hot hunger, proof of that? "What are you trying to prove?" she demanded. It took every bit of willpower in her not to clamp her hand over her crotch. Despite her efforts to the contrary, she began contracting and releasing her pelvic muscles. The rhythm wasn't doing anything to decrease her arousal. In fact, exactly the opposite was happening.

"Imprinting. So you never forget."

As if *that* was the remotest bit possible. Her feet slid forward a few inches before she could order them to stop. Now she made out his legs—his naked legs. Unfortunately, he reminded her of the famous old picture of Adam and Eve with the fig leaves.

"Are you shy?" She indicated the haze where his genitalia belonged. "Keeping your assets hidden?"

"Let your imagination take care of that."

No problem. After a moment during which she unsuccessfully tried to remind herself of the fragile line between sanity and out-and-out nuts, she walked closer on legs that felt equal parts numb and deeply alive. Her feet sank into the spongy earth, allowing moisture and muck to seep up around her toes. The sensation reminded her of a cautiously penetrating penis. The analogy would have been stronger if she hadn't suspected Laird didn't know the meaning of the word cautious, not that she'd want him to be. What was the analogy she'd come up with yesterday? It had something to do with a stallion and a mare in heat. The way he'd made her feel, it just might take a stallion with a several-foot-long cock to satisfy her—a thought that both shocked and thrilled her.

There he was. Not quite real, but with a hell of a lot more form than before. Making a lie of everything she'd ever believed about self-control.

"What are you doing?" Her nails dug into her palms. She hadn't realized she'd been so tense. "How can you do that, be not quite real?"

Not me. Something—more than me.

"Well, that makes no sense," she muttered, suddenly finding it hard to breathe.

He was forcing her to come to him. He stood there magnificently, savagely naked, his limp cock challenging her to change its condition.

"I don't want to be here," she told him. Her tone didn't carry enough weight. The weight was in her, between her legs and deep in her belly. Gnawing at her and growing ever stronger. "I don't want—damn it, I don't want you doing this to me!" Her hand fluttered near her crotch. "And don't tell me you don't know what I'm talking about."

She thought he might make fun of her. If he did, she'd punch out his lights and be done with it. Instead, she felt—kind of felt—a brush-stroke across the upper swell of her breasts. Startled, she looked down, spotted the reassuring presence of her nightgown, no hand. Yet she had no doubt that his fingers had fondled her boobs.

"I mean it! Don't."

"I don't believe you. I don't dare."

She gasped. "You're—I can hear you talking."

"Yes." He sounded as surprised as she did.

He still hadn't moved so much as a muscle. She wasn't sure he was breathing. His arms hung at his side.

Fingers—damn it, she knew what fingers felt like—slid under her garment without so much as a "by your leave". The argument could be made that she should have slapped away the intrusion, yelled about privacy and rights, threatened to call the cops, but she'd done none of those things. In truth, she couldn't think of a strong enough reason to put an end to what was happening. She'd have to be fourteen kinds of a fool not to want to play out this...this whatever it was. Only she and Laird were here, only they would ever know what took place between them. Just maybe there were no limits. If that was the case, it was possible they'd go at each other until neither of them could lift a finger. Well, she amended, maybe one well-directed finger.

Shaking off the image of two utterly exhausted people twitching their fingers at each other, she checked to see if she was still wearing anything. Yes, but for how long?

"How—" She swallowed and tried again. "How did you do that?"

"You have a woman's breasts." Proving his point, he lifted her top and cupped his phantom hands around her breasts. She stared at his buck-naked and motionless body, then down at her own. Her nightgown was bunched under her armpits, and her boobs stuck out there for the world to see. No hands covered them and yet she felt—lordy, did she!

As she stared disbelieving—but not what by any stretch of the imagination could be called unwilling—he increased his hold on her breasts until trying to pull free would hurt. They were swelling, growing ever more sensitive. Licking her dry lips, she rocked forward. He squeezed, controlled, captured. Needing to test the extent of that capture, she leaned away from the hands that surely existed only in her mind. A mammogram had nothing on this.

"You're hurting..."

He pressed his calloused thumbs against the inside of her breasts and forced them apart. At the same time, he brought the heel of his hands into play so her breasts were being lifted at the same time. "No, I'm not," he said.

He was right. Damn him. Another of her frequent fantasies had been to find herself bound and helpless while a man—always a faceless, voiceless man—roughly claimed her body. In her hallucination, she fought ropes and gag in a not-quite-desperate attempt to retain some measure of dignity, but there was no freedom from the man's mastery over her, or her carnal reaction, the powerful climax ending in unconsciousness. She tried to tell herself that today her damn imagination had gotten away from her.

But it wasn't that.

She knew it.

At least wise enough not to risk actually feeling the pain he'd called her on, she concentrated on trying to regain self-control through a series of quick, deep breaths. She succeeded only in nearly passing out from hyperventilating.

Or something else.

"You want this. Don't tell either of us that you don't," he said.

"What about you?" she challenged. He slackened his hold a

little. She still felt a world away from being free, or desiring freedom. "What do you want?"

He sighed. The sound came from low in his throat, maybe as low as his belly. She looked down at him. His penis hadn't stirred.

"Want and need are two very different things," he told her. "And I'm not sure they parallel anything either of us has ever felt before. What drives me."

"That—doesn't make sense." Her words were running together. Her muscles were turning into butter. And her breasts—

"It isn't the only thing that doesn't make sense," he mused. "I think..."

"What?"

Instead of answering, he slid his fingers to her breasts' underside and lifted until her cleavage equaled the finest cosmetic surgery. His shadow-lips brushed and covered first one and then the other nipple. He sucked, drawing her nubs between his teeth.

She gasped. Molten heat flooded her. She couldn't have felt more helpless if her arms had been staked above her, legs forced apart by knotted rope. Her cunt throbbed, begged to be filled.

"I'm learning," he whispered, "that control comes in many forms. You're my link to...to freedom. I don't dare lose that."

"By—" She was shaking. He sounded far away, as if he was speaking from the other side of a tunnel. Her thighs quivered, and her cheeks felt flushed. In her mind, she saw her labial lips swell and redden. The message was clear: I'm ready. Take me any way and any time you want. I'm too far gone to want anything else. "By taking—advantage of me?"

In her mind—damn it, just in her mind—he released her breasts only to slide his hands between her legs with enough strength that she was forced to spread them. The quivering intensified, and she couldn't have drawn away if her life depended on it. Her shorts—who knew what happened to them? He probed between her cunt's swollen lips and feathered his nails over her hot, wet clit. She gasped and panted.

"Call it what you want." His voice held at a hypnotic whisper. "I know what you need, Mala. And what I believe I must do. I just hope you can understand."

She couldn't think anymore. Nothing existed beyond his smooth, short nails and what they were doing to her. She threw back her head and raked in as much air as possible. Lifting her too-heavy arms, she flailed about until she managed to clamp them over his powerful shoulders. Gripping them for support, she widened her stance and arched her back to increase his access to her.

He toyed with her, played her like a tightly strung guitar. Or she would have called it that if she hadn't heard his own deep and none-too-steady breathing. With nails and the pads of his fingers, the base of his palms even, he left his mark, burned and branded her clit and sheath. Using his middle and forefinger, he repeatedly spread her aching folds and worked his way inside her. She rode each journey. The precipice was there—there! And then, damn it, he'd retreat, leaving her insane.

Again and again, she thrust her pelvis at him, denying him nothing. His penis would have penetrated deeper, filled her more, but this wasn't bad. Not bad at all. With every assault, her body spasmed. A climax hummed and promised. So close. On the brink. Just—just one more invasion.

"Don't," he commanded. "It isn't time for that."

"Speak—speak for yourself," was all she could manage. Her entire being centered around what his fingers ignited, fingers made slippery by her wet response.

"I'm not immune," he hissed. "I feel."

Only half conscious, she was nevertheless glad to know that. Maybe she should check his cock for verification, but she didn't dare loosen her grip on his shoulders. Couldn't think beyond being impaled, this wonderful invasion, even the damnable teasing. He couldn't possibly respect her in the morning, but what the hell did that matter? From the time she'd become sexually mature, her libido had kicked up a notch when she was ovulating, but she'd learned to accept her heightened interest in the opposite sex for the primitive signal it was and conduct herself with a semblance of dignity, not command the nearest male to ride her. But this was control lost.

"But much as I want to be part of this ride, I don't dare," he said, startling her. "I must remain in control."

Control? What the hell was that? "Whatever." She thought she had more to say, but it melted under her body's heat. Continuing to stand was more than awkward, but he was using his fingers, not some cold steel instrument. As long as his life touched hers, she'd endure.

To hell with endure. This was unadulterated torture. Sweet and strong and overwhelming, but torture nonetheless.

With two hard fingers extended as far inside her as they would go, he now spread them and tested the size of her opening. She felt swollen. Hot. Nearly boiling. Barely aware of what she was doing, she clamped down, trapping him inside her.

They breathed together. Rocked to the same rhythm, fingers pumping, clit convulsing.

No stopping. No wanting to.

Her body seemed to roar. She felt as if she was expanding and contracting at the same time, pulsing even. If he'd asked, she would have turned herself inside out. Maybe it was happening anyway. She lost the ability to breathe or focus. Blood pounded in her head. Heat flooded her cunt. Any more and she might explode. Instead, she grunted and groaned, felt a scream rake up her throat before bursting free.

Off like a rocket.

Once. Twice. Three times.

Chapter Five

Maybe upscale motels had something going for them, but as Mala sat on the side of her bed with the chunky phone on her lap and the receiver to her ear, she couldn't find a single thing to compliment about this one. It had been cleaned—sort of—and the sheets had been changed while she was gone, but she couldn't get her mind off who might have used it before her.

If it had been a couple taking advantage of time away from home and responsibility or two strangers in for a quickie, she didn't want to know about it. However, not wanting to think and shutting off the old brain were two entirely different things...especially with memories of her powerful and noisy climax still fresh in her mind. She might not remember the drive back here, but she'd never ever forget being turned into a skyrocket.

The phone's persistent ringing finally registered. No matter how long she sat here, no one was going to answer at the Clint Jaeger residence in Naples, and there was no answering machine. Muttering something she'd never want her mother to hear, she hung up, then dialed the number for Jaeger Boats. After four rings, Laird's disembodied voice informed her that he wasn't here and to leave a message. Although she was delighted to have "found" him, she didn't bother. However, she did listen to his message three more times.

Lordy but the man had a sexy voice.

She got up, wandered over to the minuscule closet and grabbed the outfit she'd chosen for her meeting with the man interested in carrying her line of jewelry. It seemed a lifetime ago that she'd given herself a headache trying to decide on the perfect ensemble. Now she couldn't care less. However, when she'd told Laird why she was here, he'd encouraged her to keep her appointment.

"I can't take over your life," he'd said as she fought, less than successfully, to bring herself back to some semblance of sanity following her powerful climax.

"No," she'd retorted. "Just my body."

She'd thought he might laugh and agree. Instead, his form had begun to shimmer and grow less distinct.

"What's happening?" she'd demanded. "What's wrong?"

"It doesn't matter."

"How can you say that? Of course it does!"

Instead of responding, he'd shrugged his unbelievably well-honed muscles. Then, slow and fading, he'd sent her another message.

"I need to get back. Learn what they want with me."

"No! It's dangerous," she'd insisted.

"I can take care of myself."

"How can you say that? You don't know what's going to happen..."

"I've always taken care of myself," he'd "said" as he faded into nothing.

Laird Jaeger, stud to the max, was a loner. She might not be sure of much that had happened since she first spotted him and his motorcycle, but she had no doubt of that.

Ralph Korn's office wasn't what she'd expected. Instead of something overflowing with arts and crafts in an older, funky part of town, the meeting took place in a third story, bare-bones office dominated by a state-of-the-art computer. As she soon learned, the computer contained a myriad of 3-D images of his clients' work. She wasn't sure how she felt about being considered a client. However, as they'd waited to be invited into the office, Sandy had assured her that that's the way successful crafts' people managed their careers these days. What better way to showcase one's work than instantly and around the world via the Internet.

"Jewelry shows particularly well this way," Ralph explained as she stared at a slowly revolving image of one of her rings. "I took the liberty of inputting a number of your pieces for your portfolio."

Ralph, who Mala guessed was about fifty and reeked of spicy cologne, leaned close. She wasn't sure his shoulder brushing hers was accidental until she glanced over at him. From the way he was looking down her cleavage, she knew it wasn't.

"You did this before I signed a contract?" she asked, determined to keep their conversation businesslike.

He clamped a scrawny arm around her shoulder. He was so close she could smell his mouthwash in addition to the cologne. Her stomach rebelled. "Mala, Mala, let's don't play games," he muttered. "You and I both know how hard it is to succeed as an independent jeweler. How many offers like mine have you had?"

None, she thought but didn't tell him. Instead, she looked at Sandy for guidance. However, Sandy only nodded from her position on the opposite side of the desk. Holding her breath, she straightened and stepped away from Ralph.

"I appreciate this," she said, although she'd dearly like to give the old fart a piece of her mind. "And you're right. Enlarging my work and giving it a 3-D quality really shows it off."

Ralph pushed the five-page contract toward her. "This is going to be successful for both of us," he said. His voice was too smooth, intimate. "Not only are you gifted, but I can market you along with your work."

"Me?" The thought of having to shake his bony hand made her slightly ill. "What do you mean?"

"You're an attractive young woman." His smile nearly split his face. He'd gone back to staring at her boobs. "I've set you up with a makeup artist and a professional photographer. Those shots will be part of the package."

"I can't afford—"

"Let's just call it my investment in you," he interrupted. "Believe me, Mala, I know what I'm doing. You want to succeed, don't you?"

"Yes, of course."

"Then let's pull out all the stops, stack the decks in our favor. You should feel flattered that you're a marketable commodity."

Much as she hated peddling herself, he had a point. Given the competition, she couldn't just sit back and let her creations speak for themselves. He told her the time and place for the photographs, and she jotted that down.

"And wear something that emphasizes your attributes." He glanced up at her, then returned his attention to her breasts.

"What a slime!" Mala exclaimed once she and Sandy were

outside. "Why didn't you warn me?"

"Because I was afraid you'd back out."

"I wish I could, but he's right. It's either play in his ballpark or—why do things have to be like this? I just want to make jewelry." *At least that had been my number one priority before he stormed into my life.*

"We've had this conversation before. Do you really want to go at it again? Look." Sandy pointed at a small cafe. "Why don't we pop in there for some coffee to celebrate? Unfortunately, it's a little early in the day for getting drunk."

Mala was wired enough that she didn't need coffee, but after everything Sandy had done, the least she could do was buy her some of the mocha she was addicted to.

"So you don't think you're going to take that dirty old man up on his not-too-subtle offer to let you jump his bones?" Sandy teased once they'd placed their order. "He's rich."

"He also gags me. That cologne—"

"You'll notice there weren't any bugs in the room. The smell knocks them dead." Sandy turned serious. "You can handle him, can't you?"

"No sweat. I can outrun him." She shuddered. "Does he think he turns me on?"

"Guys like him don't think beyond their penises." Sandy sighed. "Still, I can't help but feel sorry for him."

Mala nearly told her she'd lost her mind, then wound up agreeing with her friend. "Is he married?"

"It didn't come up. Look, I'd hate thinking I've gotten you into something that'll make you uncomfortable."

"I'll steer clear of him as much as possible. Besides, something…"

"Something what?"

Mala set down her cup and met Sandy's eyes. She frantically searched for a way to start what wouldn't sound like she'd gone over the edge, then decided she had no choice but to jump right in. "Something's happened. I don't know how to explain, how to start—how not to sound as if I've lost my mind."

"You've met a man."

"What?"

"A man. You know. Opposite sex. It's about time. I was delighted when you decided not to tie the knot with mister so-considerate-and-boring-he-makes-me-want-to-scream, but I was concerned you'd sworn off the aforementioned opposite sex."

"I did. At least I thought I had."

"Hm. Past tense here. What changed your mind?"

Careful to keep her voice low so no one could overhear, Mala told Sandy nearly everything. What she seriously downplayed was Laird's decidedly carnal impact on her. She said nothing about her heart, in large part because she didn't understand what was happening to it.

"I seriously don't know what to say," Sandy muttered when Mala ran down. "Can't think where to start."

"Do you think I'm crazy? That I've made it all up?"

"If I didn't know you as well as I do, I'd have already called the men with the butterfly nets. All right." Sandy raked her hand through her hair, picked up her cup, then set it down again. "All right. Let's assume that every word you've spoken is gospel, why did you go back out there this morning? If it was me, there's no way in hell I'd have anything to do with the joker with the motorcycle. It's just plain too spooky."

"Laird isn't spooky."

"Then what is he?"

Maybe the sexiest, most compelling man on the face of the earth. He's teaching me things about what my body's capable of that I never imagined. "Lost. He can't get back."

Sandy shook her head. "Oh boy. Oh boy. Wait a minute. Look at me."

Mala blinked. "What do you think I've been doing?"

Ignoring her, Sandy took Mala's face in her hands and peered intently. "Ah shit."

"Ah shit what?"

"You've got *that* look."

"What look?"

"Of a woman who's been royally screwed." Sandy shook her head. "How'd that happen? I thought you said he—that you didn't really see him. That he was like this ghost."

Mala wasn't sure what words she'd used.

"Say something," Sandy insisted. "I know that 'I just had my brains fucked out' look. I just wish I'd see it on my own mug more."

"He...he didn't touch me. Not really," Mala added lamely. Her face felt hot.

"Well, that explains everything." Sandy looked around as if assuring herself their conversation was still private. "What do you mean by not really?"

Mala swallowed. Then, just as she was trying to find a way to back out of what she'd said, she remembered that Sandy was her best friend.

"Maybe it's mind control," she admitted. "Well, not my mind, but I think you get the drift." Just talking about what Laird had done to her, the feel of his bold and expert fingers inside her cunt, made her squirm. From the look on Sandy's face, she had no doubt her friend understood.

"He screwed you with—with whatever?"

"Yeah."

"Shit. And you want a repeat performance, don't you? Hell, of course you do. A woman would have to be dead not to. Look, I don't want to hear any more. I envy you so much it isn't funny. Oh shit! If the two of you actually do the deed, it might kill you, but what a way to go."

"If it happens, put on my headstone that I died happy."

"What headstone? There won't be anything left of you except ashes."

Laird crouched at the edge of a pond filled with greenish water. He could barely make out his reflection, just enough to see his stubble. He felt hot and sweaty and itched from where mosquitoes had sucked at him. His feet seemed to have grown calluses overnight, allowing him to walk barefoot without discomfort. His hearing seemed keener and, even with all the vegetation, he had no trouble seeing the details of his surroundings. Even his muscles felt larger.

He was becoming whatever Night Hunter wanted him to become. No, he amended, not just Night Hunter. The others.

Laird stood and adjusted the only piece of clothing he now wore. He supposed the short, loose flap of leather was called a loincloth, not that it did that good a job. Earlier today he'd come across a bush filled with what looked like ripe fruit. Without questioning whether he'd get sick if he ate it, he did just that. Although the overly sweet fruit had briefly satisfied his hunger, his stomach now rumbled. He needed meat.

Well, he'd discovered a knife on the path...as if it had been left there for him. He could hunt. And once he'd done that, he'd listen to the insistent message in his legs that compelled him to follow the path he'd come across to its source. It might take him to knowledge.

It might also take him to a place of no return.

Could he survive that? Granted, he often felt as if he was standing on the outside of his existence and looking in, but that was the life he knew. He had a job, a roof over his head, responsibilities and dreams. A brother.

"Mala, listen to me. Feel me. Be part of this so I don't have to go through it alone."

Although he wanted to tell her about everything he'd seen and experienced, his deepest and most uncertain emotions, he only reached under the loincloth and cupped his limp penis in his palm.

"What happened between us is only the beginning. It can be more, much more. We both want that."

His penis stirred.

"You think I'm the one doing things to you, but that isn't true. I played with you, brought you to climax. Now it's your turn to return the favor. To increase the bond between us."

His cock swelled to fill his hand.

Sandy had walked to Mala's car with her. Now they stood in the tree-shaded parking lot.

"What are you going to do?" Sandy asked. "You've had your meeting with the dirty old man. Maybe you should go back to Naples. See if you can clear your head."

"Maybe," Mala muttered. "My gosh, it's hot."

"At least there's a wind."

Mala wasn't aware of a breeze. Thinking to unlock her car and get in, she pulled her keys out of her purse. Only they didn't feel like keys, more like—

"—about time. I don't know why they hire such incompetent—"

"What?" Mala interrupted. She was breathing too fast and couldn't do anything about it. "I'm sorry, I didn't..."

Laird's blood-engorged cock was even larger than she'd imagined. Its weight in her palm left no doubt of its size. It felt warmer than her hand. She longed to test its texture and contours, to run her fingertips over his balls, but she couldn't remember how to make them move.

"—a diet. I don't know how you keep it off. You weigh the same—"

"What?"

"I was paying you a compliment. Aren't you listening?"

She was trying to find the breeze Sandy had mentioned. If only the air would stir a little, she wouldn't feel as if she had a fever.

"You aren't, are you?"

"What?"

"Listening to me," Sandy insisted. "Oh my—it's happening, isn't it? He's getting to you."

Laird wiped his blood-stained hands on a leaf. Killing the wild piglet had been easier than he'd imagined. He hadn't known he could move that fast or sense where to bury the knife so death came instantly. However, without fire, he'd have to eat the carcass raw and he wasn't—yet—enough of a savage for that.

What would Mala think if she saw what he'd done?

Had he gotten through to her?

"Do you like to be on top? Maybe you want sex hard and fast. I think so, but I also think you haven't had it like that very much. That man you almost married, with him sex was civilized and circumspect. Probably you didn't scream when you came, if you came. You held back with him and tried to be a lady. I don't want a lady. I want a woman. Lusty and adventurous. I'll never sit on the sidelines or be civilized and controlled because I'm not that kind of man. When we have sex—and we will—you'll know how I like it.

"And I'll know what you need. I'll give it to you. I promise."

About to continue the discussion, Laird felt a sudden urgency that sent him down the footpath at a hard trot. He still gripped the pig carcass. After a few minutes, sweat ran off him. He wasn't out of breath, just reacting to the humid heat. His thoughts tunneled down to what his legs were doing, and he felt proud of their strength.

Nothing less than instinct told him when he reached his destination. Slowing, he walked around the last turn, angled around the last bush.

The small village was set in the middle of a large clearing. He couldn't tell whether the clearing had occurred naturally or whether the Seminole who'd made this their home were responsible.

He heard children laugh and spotted a trio of girls sitting in a circle. They stopped what they were doing and stared at him when he approached, but didn't appear either surprised or frightened.

"What are you doing?" he asked. At first the words coming from sounded like gibberish. Then he realized he'd spoken in Seminole. How he knew that he couldn't say. At least he could communicate. Without that *gift,* he'd be even more isolated.

"Playing rock-rock," the oldest girl answered. She pointed at the dead piglet. "You have been hunting."

"Yes. Are you hungry?"

The girls nodded in unison. "I am always hungry," the youngest said. "It is not a very big pig."

"No," Laird admitted. Ignoring his grumbling belly, he handed the carcass to the girls. He thought they might demur, but they jumped to their feet and ran off toward a thatched hut that was little more than a leaf roof supported by logs.

Looking around, he counted thirteen such huts. They'd been placed so close together that there was little privacy but probably the proximity of neighbors made the various families feel more secure. There was a single, large firepit in the middle of the village. Despite the day's heat, several pieces of wood smoldered. An elderly woman stirred something in a large, hollowed-out rock she'd placed at the edge of the fire. His stomach growled.

Another sound caught his attention. He cocked his head in that direction, then recognized it as a drum being beaten. He approached the sound, his legs moving in time with the rhythm. Five men sat in a semicircle around another who was responsible for the drumbeat. The drum itself appeared to be made of animal hide tightly stretched over a circular frame.

The men all looked up at the same time. Their faces were lined, their nearly naked bodies giving away their advanced age.

"You have come," one said to Laird.

Chapter Six

Damn him.

Today was as clear as the day she'd met Laird had been stormy, not that Mala gave a darn. It wasn't as if she didn't have enough to do—namely decide how she was going to deal with Ralph and the dreaded photography session. But her own agenda obviously didn't matter to Laird since he'd sent her a message with only one interpretation—namely that he needed to talk to her.

Not that talk was the right word, she amended as she approached the spot along Alligator Alley where he'd had his accident. Conversation might enter the mix somewhere along the line, but she wasn't in any mood for that until he'd taken care of other matters for her—matters that in all honesty hadn't been all-consuming until now. In fact, during the three years she'd first dated and then been engaged to Jeff Brooks, sex hadn't been a particularly important part of their relationship. Sure, she'd enjoyed slipping under the sheets with him, but she couldn't once remember being wild to jump his bones or have him do the same to her.

Today, her hot cheeks had nothing to do with the outside temperature. Neither did an undeniable heat centered in her crotch. Some people called, wrote, or sent email. Not Laird. Not that she minded all that much. After what passed for a sex life with Jeff, this torture constituted a real wake-up call. Not that she was there yet, but she had a better idea why some people became sex addicts.

"I'm here," she said as she got out of her car and walked to the edge of the wilderness. In deference to the relentless sun, she'd changed into shorts as soon as she could, following her meeting with Ralph.

Suddenly she felt a familiar hand run up the outside of her thigh. If it hadn't been for her shorts' tight fit, who knew where that particular invasion would have ended.

"Hello," she said, trying to keep her voice on an even keel. "You really know how to welcome a gal."

The bushes to her right rustled, but when Laird didn't materialize, she concluded that the breeze was responsible.

"What is it? Are you all right?" So much for her intention to keep things casual and not let him know how concerned she was for his safety. "I've had—it's been an amazing day."

She heard a car stop and turned to see a silver sedan with two young males in front.

"Car trouble, lady?" the passenger asked through his open window. "If you need help, my buddy and I'd be happy to accommodate you. If you get my drift."

"Laird," she muttered. "Now would be a good time to get out here."

Nothing, just that hand print on her thigh.

The passenger opened his door. Beyond him, she could see that the driver was giving her the once over. Great!

"Sexy lady like you shouldn't be out here all by your lonesome," the passenger informed her. "What you need is a couple of bodyguards."

"What I need is to be left alone."

"Ah, don't be like that." He exited the vehicle. There was no doubt of his message in the way he'd clamped his hand over his crotch. "I've got something in here you'd like."

"In your dreams. Do your mothers know you're out?"

His smile faded. "We're old enough. The question is, are you woman enough for us?"

This so-called conversation had gone on long enough. No matter what she said, they'd take it how they wanted.

"Go away," she ordered. "I'm not interested."

"But we are." He turned and said something she couldn't hear to the driver. Mala had felt some comfort because the driver hadn't killed the engine, but he did so now. When he opened his door, she nearly panicked. Darn but he was tall! And stronger-looking than she felt comfortable with.

Dismissing her unlocked car and purse, she practically dove for the brush. Something scratched the side of her neck, and she nearly lost her footing when she caught her shoe on an exposed root. Because she'd already been back here, she knew the brush wall became less all-encompassing a few feet beyond the side of the road. Hopefully the two jerks didn't and wouldn't be in a hurry to come after her.

"Did you see that?" she demanded of Laird. By turning her shoulders, she managed to worm her way between a couple of twenty-foot-high bushes. "For two cents, I'd punch their lights out."

Sudden realization of how the confrontation could have turned out sent a chill through her.

"They were so crude. Do they really think that approach turns women on?" She couldn't help but laugh. "On the other hand, there's your approach. You didn't ask permission. We weren't even properly introduced before you started manhandling me. Or is it womanhandling? Who cares. You know what I mean. Ah, I kind of told my best friend what we've been up to. Most people would think I need locking up, but she envies me." Mala took a deep breath, then rushed on. "Hell, I envy me. Now that I've had a taste of the wild side—"

"You are all right?"

"Yes." All of a sudden, putting more distance between herself and the two men no longer mattered. Did Laird have any idea how sexy his voice was or how much she'd wanted to hear it? "I'm all right. Where are you?"

"They're here."

"Who?" she demanded. "Those men? Make them—"

"Not them. My people."

His people? What was he talking about? Grabbing hold of a tree branch for support, she peered at her surroundings. As far as she could tell, there was no sign of him.

"I've been trying to reach your family," she told him. "The number in the Naples phone book, that's a relative?"

"No."

"Oh. But the name Jaeger isn't that common. What about the boat business? That's yours, isn't it?"

"They need me."

"Who needs you?" she asked, although she suspected he wouldn't answer. "Where are you? Why can't I see you?"

He didn't answer, but she felt his presence. It reminded her of waking up at night as a child and knowing one of her parents was in the room making sure she was all right. She didn't see Laird in the same light, and yet there was no way she could shake the conviction that he was watching everything she did. Caring about her. Protecting her if need be.

"I was going to come back," she told him. "Surely you knew that. You told me to keep my appointment. I did. But after that

I was—you didn't have to do what you did, you know." She rubbed her hand over her thigh to make her point. "I don't appreciate your proprietary approach."

"*Yes, you do.*"

She wasn't going to touch that with a ten-foot pole. "What happened? Did something—damn it, I feel like a fool talking to myself."

Another of his silences had her on the verge of screaming, but she reminded herself that she couldn't comprehend what he'd been through, or what its impact on him must be. She didn't want to think of him as being incapable of dealing emotionally with the experience, but that was a possibility.

"You're a strong man," she told him. "Brave. You'll get through this. Whatever it takes, I'll bring you back to where you belong."

Although he didn't respond to the promise she wasn't sure she could keep, she felt his approach in the earth's slight vibration. When she fully distinguished him from the patterns of sunlight and shadows, she was shocked by the change in him. It wasn't just that he looked as if he'd gone several days without shaving and was naked except for the loose and nearly inadequate fabric covering his genitals. Even with that barrier, she could tell that he was well-hung. His hair was tangled, and he had scratch marks and mosquito bites on his bronzed chest, but the transformation went beyond even that.

He now carried himself, she concluded, like a creature of the wilderness. His posture was straighter, his stride firmer. His eyes were full of wisdom about his surroundings, and she had no doubt that all his senses were on the alert. She tried not to stare at the knife fastened to the cord that held his loincloth—she couldn't think of anything else to call it—in place. There was a dark stain on his wrist that might be dried blood. She didn't think it came from him.

"You've changed," was all she could say.

"I know."

At least he was still capable of speaking English. Despite that reassurance, she couldn't ignore the accent that hadn't been there before. An alarm went off inside her. Looking at him was like looking at a jungle cat, a man-eater, a wild animal. But she couldn't run. The fierce and wild woman in her wouldn't allow that.

"Tell me about it, please."

"Not tell. Show."

Don't talk like that. It sounds—primitive. "How?"

"You will come with me."

It was an order. She'd been about to erase the distance separating them, but now it felt like walking into a lion's den. Would he attack? And if he did, would she run or meet him fang for fang?

"Why?" Her voice lacked strength. Trying to run from him would be futile, but she couldn't stop thinking about it.

"They have been waiting for me. Men, women, children, even babies."

He wasn't looking at her, not really. Instead, his attention seemed to be focused on his world. She wondered if she'd ever think of their surroundings like that.

"Who are they, Laird?"

"The Seminole."

Too much. Way too much. Her heart thundered, and her legs felt on the brink of giving out. Sanity and maybe survival itself depended on her getting back in her car, rolling up the windows, locking the doors and not stopping driving until she reached California, three thousand miles away.

Instead, she walked toward him, stopped inches from his hard, sun-heated body, reached out and placed her hand over his breast. His heart beat in there. She had to hear it pound as he fucked her. She pressed her palm against his small nipple and took some of his heat for herself. She hadn't expected him to be so hard and muscular. Most of the men she'd known had been lean white-collar types, but nothing about him felt soft. He was as wild as their surroundings, a primitive man who took what he wanted. And he wanted her as much as she did him. Forget convention and seduction. To hell with courtship! This was about sex, plain and simple.

Down and dirty and wonderful fucking.

He still wasn't looking at her. Maybe he wasn't aware of her after all...of himself as a man.

Feeling as if she was being propelled by an unknown force, she slowly and possessively ran her hands over his chest, ribs, throat, shoulder blades. Just doing that kicked her libido up a notch. She was already having trouble controlling her breathing, and as for not conjuring up images of having him locked inside her, well, forget it! He continued to stand unmoving. The memory of his control of her made her question how much he was responsible for what she was doing. It didn't matter.

She slid her hands under his arms and around to his back. That forced her closer to him. She could no longer keep him in focus. She was turning liquid from belly to hips. The inner heat rose and rose. He smelled of sweat and dirt. Far from repulsing her, the raw scents added to her arousal.

He leaned back and stared down at her, making her wonder if he was taking inventory of her. Well, she wasn't a Playboy centerfold, but then he'd never grace the cover of a romance novel. Besides, from her admittedly limited expertise, she knew that once a couple started tearing at each other, imperfections didn't matter. What she needed was an old-fashioned roll in the hay, a little bumping and grinding, some hot and—

"Kneel," he ordered.

You can't order me!

Yes, he could, she amended as her legs turned to jelly. She tried to retain her balance by leaning against him, but he grabbed her arm and pushed her away from him. He jerked down on her arms, emphasizing the command. Why should she fight? After all, she'd come here for one thing and one thing only. She sank to the ground, sliding her hands and arms down his body for support.

She felt weak, out of control.

Chapter Seven

Mala thought she detected a change in the sound the wind made, but she couldn't concentrate on it enough to be sure. It was hard to think of anything else when an all-but-naked man stood spread-legged a few inches away. A young, strong and, no doubt about it, virile man, she might add.

Her mind snagged on the word strong. Maybe because she was looking up at him, she felt just a tad overwhelmed by his size and bulk. She wasn't a ninety-eight-pound weakling, but he'd already demonstrated his mastery over her. She might fantasize about having a man overpower her, but dreams and reality were two very different things. In the real world, nothing scared her more than the thought of not being able to defend herself—to be at someone's mercy. At the same time, sticky juices pooled at her crotch and seeped down her thighs.

"Now, on your back."

Shock slammed into her chest. She felt her clit heat and swell. "My—damn it, Laird! I'm not a hooker. You can't order—"

Lifting his knee, he pressed his leg against her chest. As he did, she caught a glimpse of his swollen, enormous cock. "On your back."

Her forehead felt about to burst, but even that pressure didn't distract her from the unbelievably erotic image of her as this marvelous man's plaything. He wasn't some rapist waiting in the shadows. If her life had been in danger, she would have sensed it and fought his attempts to pull her into his world, wouldn't she? But to be possessed and at his mercy sent hot blood charging throughout her.

"I don't want..." She tried to protest with what remained of her will.

"Yes. You do."

"You're not doing this. All right, you aren't a damn brood mare. A slave."

Then why was she scooting around and stretching her legs out in front, leaning back, back until the earth pressed into her spine? Although it was so hot that the earth itself radiated warmth, she couldn't stop shivering. More fluid leaked from her. She'd become so swollen that her cunt pressed almost painfully against her shorts. It took incredible self-control not to lift her buttocks toward him like some bitch in heat.

"Spread your legs."

"Laird! What—"

"Spread them."

Inch by trembling inch, she did so. Arching her neck, she glanced at herself, relieved to discover that her shorts still covered her crotch and were absorbing her juices. At least that was what she thought until he leaned forward and sniffed. His mouth twitched and his eyes narrowed.

"I thought so," he said with what she took to be a superior tone. Then, almost tenderly, he added, "It's the way it has to be, Mala."

"I don't want—"

"Yes, you do. We both do. Wider. Open yourself to me."

Watching his expression, more than a little scared, she spread her legs as far as she could. She didn't know what to do with her hands and wound up gripping grass. Despite the thick foliage, the sun hurt her eyes, forcing her to close them to slits. She felt locked inside herself, unwilling to fully acknowledge how vulnerable she was. She heard birds, insects, herself breathing.

He was touching her, weighted thumbprints on the sensitive sides of her thighs. He'd begun at her knees, but had quickly marched toward her clitoris until maybe half of the journey had been completed. Then he slowed and painstakingly explored her soft and sensitive flesh.

Her legs trembled. She couldn't regulate her breathing. He caressed and pressed, pinched and painted. It was all she could do not to try to slap his hand away. At the same time, she felt her clit swell even more. She smelled her arousal.

Her nails dug into the earth. Pulling up handfuls of weeds, she brushed them aside only to snag more clumps. She dimly realized what she was doing mirrored the way he was handling her. Her breasts swelled within their prison until the tips felt as if they'd rip through the fabric, but, much as she needed him to work them, he wasn't done with her thighs.

Slow, so slow, he came closer to her core. As he did, her sex ached to meet his fingertips.

"Tell me," he demanded. "What do you want?"

"You, damn it."

"That doesn't tell me enough."

"Stop it!" She sounded hysterical, but couldn't do anything about it. "You haven't touched—why won't you—"

"Your shorts are in the way." Although he could have worked his fingers past the fabric, he teased her to distraction by running his nails over the flesh at the hem. Over and over again he traced the same area of skin. With each pass, he applied more pressure until she wondered if he'd draw blood.

"I'll take—them—off," she stammered.

"No, not yet."

For maybe three heartbeats she had all she could do to deal with his refusal. Only then did she realize he no longer had his hands on her.

"What are you doing?" she demanded. Frustration turned her voice ragged.

"Making you wait. Making both of us wait. Now..." Without warning, he ran two fingers under her shorts and panties. They slipped over her flooded cunt, making her sob.

"Wet," he said, "good."

"Wet doesn't begin to describe what's happening to me, damn it!" Before she could continue, disbelief snagged her breath. He'd removed his hand, robbed her of the reason to go on breathing.

"Don't do this to me!" she demanded, hating him. "Don't you damn toy with—"

"Mala! Shut up."

He backed away, grabbed her ankles and forced her legs together. "I'm running this right now. That's the way it's going to be." As if to punctuate his words, he pressed her thighs so tightly together that her swollen and sensitive cunt felt as if it was being pinched—deliciously so.

"If I let you come now," he said, "you won't remember enough of the journey. It's the trip that'll keep you with me."

"I don't care." *Liar.*

"I don't believe you. Now." He gave her thighs a final shove. "Stay like that."

Once he had her where he wanted her, Laird slowly lowered himself to a crouching position with his legs on either side of her waist—pinning and imprisoning her. She was impressed by the muscle control it had taken to accomplish that, but the feat wasn't nearly as impressive as the feel of his engorged cock brushing against her breastbone.

"What—what are you going to do?" Had she asked that before? And what made her think she needed to?

His response was to take hold of the hem of her top and pull it up to her armpits. The sudden rush of air along her ribcage brought a bit of sanity with it. He might have his way with her, but not without a fight. Determined to put her vow into action, she planted her elbows on the ground and pushed herself upward. He rocked back slightly as if willing to let her up, then grabbed her arms just above her elbows and yanked her supports out from under her. Then he dropped her onto her back again.

"You didn't have to—"

Before she could think how she should finish the sentence, he again grabbed her top and slid it up and over her breasts. She noted he was staring at them—or rather what he could see of them under the flesh colored bra. When he slid his hands over the insides of her upper arms and repositioned them over her head, she didn't try to resist. And when he again yanked at her top, she helped by lifting her back as much as possible. The garment came off. Fortunately, the groundcover felt nearly as comfortable as carpet against her back.

He leaned forward until all she could see of him was a blur, brought her hands together over her head, and held her wrists one across the other. If she put everything into it, she might have been able to wriggle out from under him, but she didn't try—not with the memory of how her earlier attempt at resistance had played out still strong.

She fought to keep her breathing regular, but it came in quick, shallow gasps. Maybe she should be afraid of him, but she wasn't...probably because she'd never felt more alive, more primitive.

Eager to feel more of him, she lifted her hips. She couldn't hold that position more than a couple of seconds, not that he gave her the chance because he lowered himself onto her, bringing her trapped wrists down and then under her breasts. He pinioned them there with his left hand which left his right free to slide under the top of her bra. He cupped first one breast and then the other, all the time staring at her so intently that she closed her eyes to escape his intensity.

From inside her self-imposed prison, she took stock. His weight pinned her from her hips down, and his left hand was so large that it easily handcuffed her wrists. In addition, he'd leveraged his weight so she could barely move her upper body. She could, as if it made any difference, move her head from side to side and bend her knees. She didn't try.

She was his prisoner, plain and simple. If he wanted to massage her breasts and mold them into contours of his choosing, he'd do it. If he chose to clamp his fingers around her throat and squeeze the life out of her, she wouldn't have been able to stop him.

For reasons she wasn't about to explore, that excited her.

Still holding her in place, he slipped his hand out from under her bra, then around behind her where he deftly unhooked it. He couldn't yank it off without releasing her wrists, but obviously that didn't matter to him.

With her eyes still shut, she imagined him staring at her breasts and taking their measure. They weren't half bad, not as magnificent as those that had been artificially enhanced, but genetics had been kind to her. Maybe he agreed, because this time when he laid claim to them, it was with a new tenderness—or if not tenderness, a certain consideration.

Consideration for her response.

He touched and tasted, took a nipple between thumb and forefinger much as she'd recently claimed his. He had more to play with than she'd had. And was better at it.

Once again moisture flooded her cunt and added to what was already there. Her nipples hardened, and she sucked in humid air through flared nostrils. He spread his fingers over the outside of her breast and pushed inward, then placed his palm over the small mountain he'd created and created indentations with his rough finger pads. Done with that, he rolled her swollen and sensitive nipple back and forth, back and forth, creating enough friction to be almost painful.

She felt her hips lifting off the ground again, tried to spread her legs. She sobbed in frustration because they remained clamped together and imprisoned by his legs. How could he thrust his cock into her if he trapped her like this? If she still had on shorts and panties? Didn't he know how frustrated she was becoming, how she desperately needed him filling her?

Although she wasn't sure she had the courage for this, she opened her eyes. He stared down at her, but she couldn't guess what he was thinking. He looked—not impassive really but something she couldn't reach or comprehend. Wild.

Determined.

"I'm not—I'm not going to run away," she managed, although it might be a lie. "Please, let me up. Get these damn clothes off me."

"No."

"Why not?"

"It is better this way."

For which of us? Certainly not for her, and she couldn't imagine he was satisfied with endless foreplay. If he was into control, he shouldn't have any complaints, but his cock couldn't possibly get any larger. Surely he wanted to shove it in her.

Determined to get her point across, she resorted to rhythmically lifting her hips toward him. Each thrust lasted only a second because she wasn't sure how long her back would hold out. Still, again and again, she pressed her pelvis bone against the inside of his thighs. It would have been impossible if he rested his full weight on her, but he'd repositioned himself so his knees bore that responsibility.

She could only imagine what it felt like to have that damnable fabric repeatedly brush the tip of his swollen penis. Fortunately, her imagination was vivid—that and what her repeated thrusting was doing to her. Sex without penetration pretty much summed it up—sex with her doing the pumping. Her pussy hot and humming.

He growled, and she answered with a throaty moan.

"It—doesn't have to be—like this." Spent, she rested. In her mind, she continued her erotic thrusts, but that would have to suffice until her buttocks muscles recovered. "We can do this—another way."

Did panthers purr? She didn't think so, and yet the sound that came from his throat prompted the question.

"You've made me wait—so long. Teasing. Turning me inside out. I deserve—" She tensed in preparation to start pumping again. "More than this."

Instead of agreeing or disagreeing, he leaned forward and lowered himself onto her, trapping her arms between them. His cock now pressed against her belly, the tip grinding into her navel—or it would have if it hadn't been for the two layers of fabric. She wanted to concentrate on that, but couldn't because he'd started nipping her jaw line and the side of her neck. She could only imagine what he looked like with his butt sticking up in the air to accommodate his greater length to hers. Instead of needing to laugh, she found the image erotic—not that she needed more in that department. Trusting and yet not, she turned her head to the side and gave him full access.

He closed his mouth around the taut tendon at the outside of her neck. She had no doubt that the strength in his jaw was enough to kill her. Not pain, not really. On the edge, between pleasure and discomfort.

A little heat had gone out of her flooded passage when she stopped her gyrations, but now the fire returned. Only one thing would quench it—him inside her.

"Fuck me!" she gasped. "Laird, do it!"

If he heard, he gave no indication. Instead, he continued to nibble almost playfully at her neck. His cock felt heavy against her belly, and she'd become aware of the texture and weight of his balls.

"Please!"

Snarling, he scrambled off her, planting his feet under him and standing. Before she could react, he reached down, grabbed her shoulders and hauled her up with him. Her bra straps started slipping off her arms. She grabbed the garment and tore it from her. Before she could turn her attention to her shorts, he took charge by yanking the elastic waistband down her hips. The elastic caught around her thighs, but only for a moment because, impatient with his speed, she pulled them off the rest of the way. She reached for her panties, but he caught her hands and pushed her away from him. His gaze seared her.

"Well?" she managed. "Do you like what you see?"

"You are a woman."

Woman. Talk about summoning it up with a single word. "I-I wasn't sure," she admitted. "For too long—I was in a relationship that didn't—that never did this to me."

"Today is different?"

She swayed, felt lightheaded. "Today's different from anything I've ever done in my life."

He continued looking at her, staring at her face for a long minute before raking his gaze lower. She felt the heat of that stare on her throat and then her breasts. Finally he turned his attention to her waist and belly. Suddenly shy, she tried to cover her crotch with her hands, but her arms were so heavy. Besides, she still wore that tiny piece of white nylon and lace.

But not for long, she amended as he jerked his head at her, commanding her to come to him. She did so mindlessly, and when she stood before him, he took hold of the front of her panties and tugged. They too hung up on her hips, prompting her to suck in her breath to aid in the disrobing, but once the scrap of cloth was at the juncture between hips and legs, she let him take over again. He crouched, rolling the garment down her legs. She stepped out of it.

Naked before him. Finally.

Now what? she asked herself. *Think, damn it. Now what?*

Despite the way her fingers trembled, it didn't take long to untie the knot of cord over his hip that held the loincloth in place and toss it away.

Bigger than she'd imagined.

Her tongue snaked out to touch her upper lip. She didn't even try to pretend she wasn't mesmerized by the contours and veins of his engorged penis and heavy testicles.

"You're—magnificent."

He didn't respond, didn't move.

"You—you belong inside me. Now, now!"

Still wordless, he clamped his hands around her waist,

propelled her over to a rotting tree stump covered with moss and ferns, and backed her against it. Not waiting for him to position her, she reached behind and found a handhold. Then she arched away from him, spreading her legs and thrusting her pelvis at him at the same time. After staring at her from under hooded eyes, he lifted her so her toes barely touched the ground. Because there was an indentation in the ground at the front of the stump, he could stand in it—make the fit of cock to cunt perfect.

Now! Now before I lose my everlasting mind!

Using his thumbs, he spread her hot, wet folds. She felt the first exquisite kiss of cock against swollen bud, trembled.

"No!" a stranger ordered.

Fighting terror, she forced herself to concentrate. Laird had stepped away from her. Something about his stance made her question whether he had any control over what he was doing.

"Laird?"

Teeth bared, his fists raised and at the ready, he turned. Everything about him said he was facing an adversary, a foe, maybe danger, but she didn't see anything or anyone.

"Laird? What is it?" she demanded. "Who..."

He crouched slightly as if readying himself for attack.

"No," he said, the word half defiance, half plea. "No."

What are you talking about? Because she didn't dare distract him, she simply settled herself back onto her feet and watched, waited. She couldn't begin to ignore her sexual frustration, couldn't bring herself to close her legs.

Laird looked no less wary than he had a moment ago, and she read denial in every line of his body, but he was no longer ruled by shock. Instead, she could swear he accepted something she couldn't begin to comprehend. When he spoke, she couldn't understand a word. The only thing she had no doubt of was that he was talking to someone—someone she couldn't see.

Slowly, as if he couldn't put his mind fully on the task, his fingers relaxed, and he no longer put her in mind of a trapped animal. He straightened and another look—peacefulness or acceptance—came over him.

Then he walked away from her. Let the Everglades embrace him.

"Laird!" she screamed.

Nothing.

"Laird!"

Still nothing.

It was night by the time Mala let herself into her small home in Naples. The inside air was stale, prompting her to open windows before checking her answering machine. When she did, she found that Ralph Korn had left two messages, both emphasizing how much he admired her work and hinting at a personal relationship.

After deleting the messages, she walked into her bathroom, stripped off her Everglades-soiled clothing, and stepped into the shower. Scrubbing off the day's sweat felt wonderful, as did shampooing her hair twice.

Then, instead of turning off the water, she ran her washcloth between her legs. Frustration guided her fingers into her opening, but the moment the rough fabric touched her need-swollen bud, she groaned and rested her shoulder against the shower wall.

Self-satisfaction wouldn't do the trick tonight. Only Laird—

or Thunder—would. And until she understood what had happened to him, until she truly believed he was all right, she couldn't think of anything else.

She slowly dried herself, her fingers lingering over her still-sensitive breasts and the belly that remembered the feel of his bulging cock. Despite her satisfaction, however, certain things about their encounter bothered her. Only by steeling herself against raw memories was she able to acknowledge what it was. The man she'd mated with had been primitive and uncivilized, not the lonely-eyed motorcyclist she'd seen so long ago. She wanted him to be both, pure male animal and filled with humanity.

Once she'd pulled on a nightshirt, she thumbed through the phone book, looking for the number for Clint Jaeger. She didn't care that it was going on for ten p.m. One way or the other, she'd get some answers or—or what?

A man answered after the fourth ring. As he said "hello", she strained to catch a similarity to Laird's voice, but how could she when the last time she'd heard her phantom lover, he'd been speaking in Seminole?

"Hello," she responded, hoping she didn't sound like a telemarketer. Before the man could cut her off, she explained that she was trying to contact someone who knew Laird Jaeger. "Are you related to him?" she asked. "I know it's late, but this is important. He might be in trouble."

"Lady, believe me, my brother's middle name is trouble."

Laird's brother! "I wouldn't know about that," she stammered. No matter what she said, it would sound insane. "He owns a motorcycle, doesn't he?"

"The way I see it, the cycle owns him."

"Not anymore," she blurted.

"Huh? Did you buy it from him? Nah, no matter how broke

he might be, he wouldn't get rid of it."

"He didn't have a choice."

After taking a deep breath in a not-too-successful attempt to calm herself, she blurted out, not everything, but enough to let Clint know that Laird had been in a motorcycle accident that had propelled him into the Everglades. He was still there.

"What the hell are you talking about?" Clint demanded. "He's done some damn reckless things in his life, but getting lost isn't one of them. Look, lady, I hate to break it to you, but my brother attracts broads like fish to live bait. He doesn't give a damn about any of them beyond the obvious. If you're looking to hook up with him, you're going to have to do better than this cock-and-bull story."

"You don't believe me? I'm serious." She felt on the verge of tears and suspected it showed in her voice. "Why would I make up something like that?"

Clint didn't immediately answer. "What do you want from me?" he asked. "If you're on the up and up, this is a matter for the police."

"They don't believe me," she blurted and was instantly sorry. "I thought—you're his brother. Please, help me find him."

There was more dead air time, and then Clint cleared his throat. "I was half asleep when you called. I'm still trying to put it together. Besides, if you're right about—I gotta tell you it makes no sense."

"I'm not lying. Why would I?"

"I don't know you, lady, so I'm not going to comment on that. But let's say that my brother got himself lost. We can't go looking at night, can we?"

"No," she admitted. Besides, now that she was talking to Clint, she was having second thoughts about her half-baked plan to convince someone who should love Laird to help her free him from what or who had him. "But at daylight—"

"At dawn I'll be at his business trying to hold it together. Meet me there."

Chapter Eight

Mala might have dozed off a few times during the night, but she certainly didn't feel as if she had. Her exhaustion was a combination of concern for Laird's welfare, what she'd have to do in order to convince his brother that he was in trouble, and sexual frustration. Unfortunately, she couldn't do a thing to minimize any of those conditions.

It was still technically dawn when she pulled into the small but upscale marina that looked out at the calm, pristine Gulf of Mexico. A few people were stirring, prompting her to wonder if they'd slept onboard. The majority of the craft moored in slips near the parking area were well beyond the budget of the middle class, and she had visions of wild parties attended by the rich and beautiful. She couldn't imagine Laird being part of that scene, but really, what did she know about him?

A discreet sign pointed toward several water-oriented businesses, and she cautiously made her way along a long wooden walkway paralleling the shore. Laird's business was at the end of the walkway and appeared to consist of two well-maintained open, flat-bottomed boats equipped with fishing gear and chairs. Having gone fishing only a few times in her life and finding it boring, she couldn't say what kind of fish the equipment was designed to catch. Docked a short distance from the fishing boats and storage-shed-sized office was a well-designed, handmade white-and-blue houseboat with a deck and railing along two sides. Several lounge chairs had been fastened to the deck floor. A person—Laird—could live there. She couldn't shake the thought that he might never return.

She was heading toward the little office when the door opened and a man a good six inches shorter than Laird wearing carefully pressed slacks and a nearly new white shirt stepped out. His shiny black shoes appeared ill-equipped for standing up against salt water. Although she set his age at mid-thirties, he carried a spare tire and was going bald. His somber expression didn't change when he saw her.

"You called last night," the man said without preliminary, folding his arms over his belly. "It was you, wasn't it?"

She nodded. "I'm sorry I woke you, but I couldn't think of anything else to do."

"Hm. Look, Laird's got customers coming in a few minutes, and I'm going to have deal with them, so let's cut to the chase. Tell me again what happened."

She did as he ordered, this time detailing every moment of the accident in the middle of a rainstorm, the police search, her forays into the Everglades. His expression remained impassive, but she had no doubt he was scrutinizing her intently. She couldn't bring herself to tell him she'd actually seen Laird, nearly become his lover.

"How did you know his name?"

That brought her up short. "I—I found his wallet." Why had she lied?

"I don't think so."

"That's your decision," she insisted. "He's missing, isn't he? Don't you care what happens to him?"

Clint Jaeger nodded. "Yes, I do. Let me tell you a few

things. First, I work in the district attorney's office. Mostly I push papers around, but that gives me access to certain pieces of information. Not only that, I know a lot of cops."

Dread tightened her stomach.

"After you hung up, I made some calls. I got a hold of the officer who led the so-called search. They found no sign of Laird, let alone any indication there'd been a motorcycle accident."

He wasn't going to help. Nothing else mattered.

"Lady, I don't know what kind of scam you're trying to pull. But—"

"I'm not! He's missing, isn't he? You can't deny that."

"No, I can't. However, despite my brother's obvious physical attributes and charm with the ladies, he's always been restless. Always searching. With good reason. I wouldn't put it past him to take off, go try to find himself. Maybe you pushed, and he decided to bail before you got any closer. He needs his space."

"What do you mean by 'with good reason'?" she demanded. At any moment Clint might order her to leave. She had to take advantage of anything he told her.

Clint patted his belly. "I'm assuming you noticed that Laird and I don't look alike. That's because we aren't related."

Mala could only blink and try not to let her mouth sag open.

"But we were raised together," Clint supplied before she could form a question. "In the same foster home."

Clint's brief and unemotional story nearly tore her apart. Because the two rootless boys had had no one else to rely on or trust, Laird and Clint had shared endless confidences. As a result, Clint knew Laird had been four or five when he'd been taken from his parents and made a ward of the state. He'd bounced from home to home until he was in the third grade and joined the household where Clint already lived. By then, Laird's parents had lost all legal claims to him. He didn't remember what they looked like, where they came from—even their names.

"Once we'd grown up, I told him to demand to have his records opened so he'd at least have some roots, but he said that if his parents didn't want him, he'd close that chapter to his life. The name he goes by—it isn't the one he was born with."

"It—isn't?" Her heart bled for the homeless boy Laird had once been.

"Apparently, his last name was changed every time he went into a new foster home. Maybe those people wanted him to think he belonged. When he came to where I was and learned I'd taken those people's surname, he asked to have his legally changed." Clint shrugged. "His birth parents had no say in that. As for his first name—he had a teacher he admired called Laird."

She heard approaching footsteps on the wooden walkway but didn't turn to see who was coming. Instead, she stared at the gentle waves lapping against the sides of the fishing boats—boats Laird made his living by.

"Is it possible," she asked. "That his mother and father were Indian? Seminole?"

Why didn't you tell me any of this? Did you think I wouldn't care? I do. My God, I do.

Mala had driven less than a mile before she admitted she was in no shape to be behind the wheel. The boulevard she was on had been constructed within sight of the bay, and she pulled over at a restaurant with an incredible view of water and sky. A few minutes later, she sat at a small outside table, sipping coffee and staring absently at seagulls and other birds as a few sailboats slid past.

Did Laird ever go sailing? She easily imagined him working the ropes so the sails caught the wind to best advantage, but the image became even stronger when she allowed her thoughts to return to the Everglades.

"Yes," Clint had answered her. He and Laird had speculated that Laird's dark coloring and midnight hair and eyes spoke of Indian heritage. Because he had no memory of living anywhere except Florida, Laird wondered if his parents were Seminole.

The Seminole now had him. Were changing him in ways she couldn't comprehend but held her spellbound.

She shuddered and brought her coffee cup close to her face, trying to warm herself from the steam. She couldn't be cold, not on a day that might reach a hundred degrees. But, considering everything she'd learned this morning, how could it be otherwise?

"You haven't touched me today," she "told" him. *"Why not?"*

Maybe, she thought, she'd been so intent on what she'd been doing since getting up that her body hadn't been receptive to his particular mode of communication. She concentrated on her nerves and muscles, even the blood pulsing though her veins. She felt surprisingly alive for someone who was sleep deprived. But sexual energy, although part of the mix, wasn't overwhelming.

"Where are you?" she asked. *"It scares me when I don't hear from you. Are...are you all right?"*

Her vision blurred, but although she loved the setting, she didn't try to bring it back into focus. Instead, she went deep inside herself and found remnants of Laird.

More than remnants.

He was awake. Sitting, not walking. Naked. Surrounded by somber-faced Seminole men of all ages. One of the young men had been wounded, and despite the bandages around his chest, she could tell the wound was infected. The three oldest faces were etched with deep lines so they looked haggard. In contrast, Laird appeared, not exactly peaceful, but accepting. He'd been staring at the long-bladed knife he held, but now he looked up.

An elderly man stepped out of the shadows and slowly, solemnly approached Laird. The newcomer was lean to the point of gauntness but carried himself with pride. He wore a bright blanket-like garment she assumed denoted some kind of ceremony. As he passed each of the men surrounding Laird, they held out their hands. He nodded and spoke quietly to them in turn. He held something so small she couldn't tell what it was. He seemed gentler, less on edge than he'd been yesterday. She hoped he was more at peace with himself and his surroundings—surroundings that had wrapped an unfathomable hold on her.

As she'd known he would, the old man finally positioned himself in front of Laird and said something in Seminole. Laird replied and got to his feet. He towered over the older man, but deferred to him. The others began chanting. Although she didn't understand a word of what they were saying, she found herself getting caught up in a rhythm that reminded her of the Everglades' song. Even Laird swayed in time. The chanting seemed to go on for a long time, but she was in no hurry to have it end.

She remained vaguely aware of activity around her, the clink of silverware, laughter, someone calling out from one of the sailboats, her coffee growing cold, but it would take a lot more than that to distract her.

At length the singers fell silent, and all eyes turned to the elderly man in the bright costume. He reached up and placed a hand on Laird's shoulder. After nodding at every member of the audience—she couldn't think what else to call them—Laird dropped to his knees and held out his hands the way the others had earlier.

Despite the deep shadows, she could see the old man smile as he placed something over Laird's head and positioned it at his throat. Laird briefly clasped his hand over the object and then stood again so everyone could see.

He now wore a small leather bag decorated with shells. A slender leather cord held the bag in place.

"I don't know when I'll be back," she told Clint. "But I'll call when I have something to tell you."

"You're going alone?" he asked. The phone connection was poor, but she still noted concern in his voice.

"Yes. It's—it's the way it needs to be."

"I can't say whether you're right or not. Be careful."

"Careful? I thought you didn't believe your brother disappeared in the Everglades."

He sighed. "I'm not sure what I believe. He isn't at work. He hasn't been home. And he hasn't called me."

It struck her as sad that only a foster brother cared what happened to Laird, but he'd probably deliberately kept things that way. If that was so, if he'd never developed close ties, why had things changed with her?

After hanging up, she went into her bedroom and changed into jeans shorts and a cotton shirt. She put on her most comfortable pair of tennis shoes and dug a seldom-used backpack out of her closet which she filled with a change of clothes for herself and a shirt and sweat pants Jeff had left behind after they'd broken up. The outfit would be snug on Laird, but as far as she knew, the only thing he now had to his name was that loincloth. He couldn't return to civilization dressed like that.

Feeling as if she'd come home, Mala slipped into the Everglades. It was still morning, but hot enough that most of the mosquitoes had gone into hiding. Still, she was glad she'd remembered to bring along repellant since she had no idea how long she'd be here this time—or whether she'd return alone or with Laird.

"I'm back," she said aloud. "I wasn't sure I would be. Your arguments for keeping me near you are, shall we say, powerful. But that scares me."

She fell silent as she searched for the now-familiar trail, then trudged on once she'd found it. The pack on her back made it sweat.

"I thought—after I left the last time I was sure you'd use your, ah, persuasive powers on me. But you haven't. Why? Don't you need me anymore?"

He didn't respond or materialize and she couldn't sense his presence.

"I find that hard to believe," she said, shocked by the desperation in her voice. "I told your brother what happened, but I don't know if he believes me. He cares about you. I want you to know that."

Something about the air changed. Maybe a predator—

"Are you here? I—I've been thinking. Whatever the hold over you, it's getting stronger. I saw—don't ask me how—I saw a ceremony in which an old man placed a leather bag around your neck. It looked as if it was full. What's the significance? Please, I'd like to know."

"You do not belong here."

Thank God! Stopping, she looked around but saw nothing. "What—what do you mean?"

"What has happened does not concern you."

"No! You're wrong. Laird?" she called out when he didn't respond. The backpack pressed into her shoulders, and she shrugged out of it and dropped it to the ground. "I wouldn't be here if you weren't important to me. You didn't, you know, get to me sexually."

"I did not try."

"Because you had other things on your mind. I understand." The word understand swirled around her, becoming more complex with every heartbeat. "If lust was the only thing holding us together, I wouldn't be here. But I am. And you know why."

The feeling that he'd come closer intensified.

"I talked to your brother," she said. "The man you consider your brother. He told me about your upbringing." She paused, gathering courage. "You've never felt you belonged anywhere. You've always been looking for—for something. Now you think you've found it."

The Everglades surrendered its hold on him. She sensed the wilderness's struggle and the strength it took for Laird to free himself. Once again he'd changed since the last time she'd seen him. He still hadn't shaved and the elements had roughened his flesh even more. His muscles seemed to have grown, perhaps in preparation for what might be ahead of him.

She didn't know whether he wore the same loincloth. The shell-decorated leather bag rested against his chest, looking for all the world as if it belonged there.

Acknowledging the heat in her cunt, her hardened areolas, she indicated his necklace. "What does it mean?"

"My legacy."

Her mouth opened but nothing came out. She tried to meet his gaze, but was suddenly afraid of what she'd find in his eyes.

"I belong here," he said.

No! "How can you say that?" she demanded, although she'd thought that herself when she'd *seen* him with the Seminoles. He hadn't moved since he'd revealed himself, but that didn't stop her from sensing him. Wanting him with a ferocity that rocked her. She could jump this man, ram him deep, deep inside her and ride him until they both passed out. "You've spent years building a life in Naples. I saw your business, your boats. You live in that houseboat, don't you? You built it."

"Yes."

Her body began to hum. She felt more at peace than she had in a long, long time. Her pussy softened and swelled. She couldn't stop the memories of what had happened the last time they were together.

"I'm in awe of your skill," she said, although she could no longer remember why she'd thought it was so important to ground him in reality. In truth, she was losing touch with reality herself. "You—you enjoy sitting out on your deck, don't you?"

"I speak Seminole."

"I, ah..."

"The words are in me. They have always been."

He was magnificent! There was no other way to describe it.

And if she didn't mate with him, now, she'd spend the rest of her life regretting it.

"They need me."

"So do I," she blurted. "Laird—Thunder—the things you've done to me—" Not giving herself time to think about what she was doing, she ran her hands over her breasts, flattening them and then grabbing the nipples as best she could. Her lips felt numb. In contrast, she was aware of every cell of her body from belly to crotch. Her nerve endings felt hot and almost as if they'd been scraped with sandpaper. Thrown off balance by her sudden, deep response, she fought to remember the world she'd left behind, but it no longer existed.

Only he did.

Only completing what they'd begun earlier mattered.

"Are you doing *it* again?" she managed. "You are, aren't you?"

Chapter Nine

Mala didn't know what to expect. She tried to recall what had happened between them before and draw on that, but it was nearly impossible to think about anything except this moment. His body.

It was as if he was challenging her to touch him. Did he think she lacked the courage?

Maybe, she admitted. He was no longer a motorcycle-riding, houseboat-living, self-employed fishing guide. He'd become part of a beleaguered people from the past—a past that had embraced him and now touched her.

Touch. Yes. That's what this was about.

"What is it like with the Seminoles?" she asked to distract herself and maybe him from the fact she was walking toward him. Someone had interrupted them before. Was that person watching, ready to interrupt once more? If so, he'd have a hell of a fight on his hands from her. "Did they offer you a beautiful virgin?"

"No."

"A pity. A lot of men would die happy if they had that."

"I am not a lot of men." He turned his attention to her legs as if to let her know she hadn't fooled him. He knew her intention. "I would not take a child."

"I'm glad to hear that." She meant it. "But I'm not a virgin."

Something that might become a smile twitched the corner of his mouth. He was right. She'd proven beyond a doubt she had experience in that department. She thought about letting him know what had brought her here—her determination to do everything possible to return him to the world he'd grown up in—but she didn't want to show her hand and risk him walking away from her. The thought of having to endure another day of intense sexual frustration nearly took off the top of her head. No way, no how!

"You've gotten under my skin with your rather unique techniques," she admitted. "Made it nearly impossible for me to think of anything else." Just the idea of touching him made her fingers burn, but if she didn't take this, whatever it was, slow and retain some self-control, she could lose herself in him. Hadn't it already happened? Not that she was complaining. She just needed more. "I couldn't just let it end."

"I did not forget you."

"Didn't you? You didn't try to reach me."

He fingered his necklace. "There was no time."

"But you came to me now."

He nodded.

"For how long?" How much longer could she stand here talking to him? From the message in her newly heavy breasts and the hot dampness between her legs, not much. "When—when do you have to return?"

"They will let me know."

"They?"

"The elders."

So that's what they were called. "I saw—I saw one of them give you that necklace. It was like this—I don't know, kind of a dream I had." Sweat glistened on his chest. If she ran her tongue over it— "They know you're here, with me, don't they?"

He gave a dismissive shrug.

"I've never met anyone like you." *How corny could she get?* "You can't blame me for being—" She bit down to keep the word obsessed from escaping. "Are you getting enough to eat?" That wasn't much better, but thinking was getting harder and harder. Her entire body felt alive, on fire.

"The children need food more than I do."

Concentrate! Don't lose—yourself. She could remind him she hadn't seen the village, and did he really expect her to believe everything he told her about the Seminole, but her vision of the ceremony had been so vivid. And he wore the necklace.

Taking courage in hand, she touched the small, perfect shells. They carried his warmth. "I'm always influenced by seashells when I'm creating jewelry," she said softly. "I love the soft colors, the tiny variations. They're so fragile and yet..."

He hadn't removed her hand from what was maybe sacred to the Seminole. And when he took a deeper-than-usual breath, she told herself that her nearness had gotten to him. She struggled for composure.

"The last time we were together," she said. "You did what you wanted to me."

"What I needed to."

He was looking down at her. How could something so ordinary feel so erotic?

"It turned me on."

"I know."

Of course he did. "Right up to the end when it all came crashing to an end. It was everything a woman could ever want.

You played me like a harp. I felt, hell, like I'd become your plaything. Maybe I didn't like everything you did but—all right, I got off on every second of it, but I don't want it to be like that today."

She thought he tensed, but couldn't be sure.

"You're bigger than me. So much stronger. Sometimes that scares me."

"Does it?"

He hadn't apologized, didn't even seem particularly concerned. "You don't know what that's like, do you? It's easier for a man, having greater strength and all."

Was she babbling? The truth was, part of what had nearly driven her over the edge had been the difference in their strengths. In today's dog-eat-dog world, there was something terribly erotic and exciting about being sexually dominated.

Her arm began to ache, and she reluctantly released the bag. Only then did she remember that it was full. What was in it? Maybe, sometime, she'd learn.

"Women always—women have to take that in consideration when they're with a man," she continued. "Will we be safe? Can this man be trusted?" Did she care or was she willing to do whatever it took to have him bury his cock inside her?

"Do you trust me?" He held up his hands as if asking her to judge them.

"Should I?"

"No."

No. Damn him for speaking the truth. Although her parents would have locked her in her room and thrown away the key if they'd known what she was doing, she took his hands and brought them near her breasts. The thought of his fingers exploring their heat and weight was all it took to tighten her nipples so they pressed against her bra, their aroused state obvious. "Then I won't," she said.

"Good."

He cupped his hands over her breasts, but although they fit perfectly within his embrace, he went no further than that. Hating the damn blouse and bra, eager for more, she reached up and ran her fingers over his jaw. Although she couldn't completely ignore the heat between her legs, most of her attention was focused on her heavy, swollen breasts.

"How many women have been in your bedroom?" she asked.

"I do not know."

Her breasts felt sheltered, protected. She wanted to look down at his penis to see what was going on there, but didn't.

"More than you can count?"

"That is the past, Mala."

She wanted to believe him, but she needed reassurance that she was different from all those other women. She was, darn it. None had followed him into the Everglades. None knew what had happened to him or how fragile was his tie with the real world. Surely he'd never made an erotic mental condition with them and turned them into mindless sex addicts. If he had, they would have followed him into the Everglades.

That's why she'd come here, she reminded herself. To rescue him. To keep him with her. Because she couldn't imagine life without him. The world beyond him held no meaning.

Leaning forward, she kissed the space between his breasts, savoring flesh, muscle, and bone. He clamped a hand around her throat.

"Don't do that," she warned. "I've gone through too much to

stop now. Surely you know that."

"This isn't a game."

"Like I don't know that? What is it? Something..."

Holding her head immobile, he studied his surroundings. She did the best she could to duplicate his actions, fear nibbling at her.

"It's all right," she told him although of course she didn't know that. "Laird, please, we need and deserve to live in the moment. To do what we both want."

He didn't argue, and when he relaxed his grip on her, she kissed his chest again, then licked her lips and tasted his sweat. Needing more, she ran her damp tongue around the outside of his left breast. The salty taste only made her hungry for more. Switching to his right, she slowed her exploration and drew out the journey.

His skin was smoother than she'd expected, an exciting contrast to the hard muscles underneath. She felt her cunt twitch and boldly acknowledged it by reaching between her legs and rubbing herself through the fabric there. The crotch of her panties slipped easily over her flesh, proof that her juices were flowing. She was ready, ready, willing and beyond eager to be invaded.

For a moment, her thoughts again snagged on the male voice that had called him from her side before. Whoever that had been might be watching.

It didn't matter because words like invaded, penetrated, speared, but most of all fucked hammered at her.

Before he could grow accustomed—or heaven forbid—bored with what she was doing, she turned her head sideways and nibbled at his nipple. At first she toyed with him, tested and teased while he roughly massaged her boobs, but all of a sudden, her body flamed, causing her to nip the puckered nub.

He jerked away, but before she felt the loss, he released her so-sensitive breasts and planted his widespread hands over her buttocks. He pulled her toward him until their pelvises were pressed together, leaving no doubt of his arousal.

Fumbling a bit because with her face a scant inch from his chest she couldn't see what she was doing, she unfastened his loincloth. His fingers dug into her butt cheeks, imprisoning her against him. Unless he ordered her to stop—and maybe even if he did—she'd continue her seduction.

Maybe she was going at it all wrong. She loved to be romanced and seduced, and there was a great deal to be said about getting to know a man before jumping into bed with him, but although she didn't know a great many things like the size of his bank account, what his favorite time of day was, whether he wanted children, what made him laugh or cry, those things didn't matter. They wouldn't until after they'd become lovers. Lovers? What she needed and suspected he did too was a lot earthier than that.

Her neck ached a little from the way she had to turn her head in order to again take his nipple between her teeth, but it was worth it. Whew, was it! This was supposed to be about her getting to him, but even more liquid heat flowed into her throbbing clit. Unfortunately, she could no longer reach herself there. She'd give anything to have his cock fill her!

Ignore it, somehow.

Concentrating or at least trying to, she slid her hands down his thighs and took possession of his hard cock. At first, the feel, weight and promise of the swollen shaft stopped her. With this simple and complex organ, he could satisfy her, blow her mind. If she did things right, she could make him forget every other woman he'd ever known. Vowing to do that, she cupped both hands around the shaft and twisted slightly, creating friction. After a few seconds of that—a few seconds of his fingernails digging into her buttocks as if trying to reach clear through to her heated clit—she abruptly stepped back and spun away from him.

"Don't," she warned when he moved to come after her. *Shit! This was supposed to be about him, for him! But my body—* "Don't move. Just stand there."

She thought he might ignore her, but he seemed content to remain where he was with his cock at full attention and his eyes riveted on her. Aware of her every movement, trembling and weak in the legs, she pulled her shirt over her head. Then she flung it from her and reached for her bra hooks. *Him, not you! Don't forget that!*

"This is going to take time," she whispered. She barely remembered how to speak.

She couldn't be sure if he'd heard, but maybe it didn't matter because, truth be known, he couldn't jump her bones fast enough. She was crazy making that kind of promise. She'd once gone to a bar advertising *Girls, Girls, Girls, All Nude* with friends. Fortified by drinks, they'd laughed themselves silly watching strip acts, but despite the haze of booze, she'd remembered some of what the girls had done to turn on the paying male customers.

One thing had stood out. They'd never once stopped moving, never risked letting the men's attention wander. The strippers had seemed to enjoy themselves, but she couldn't be sure about that. She had no such doubts about her own reaction. Even with everything she had to concentrate on, her skin was getting tight as if her blood supply was becoming too great to be contained. Had she been born for this moment with this man?

Rotating her hips and shoulders at the same time—

something the stripper had done effortlessly—took unbelievable concentration, enough so the inner heat she'd been battling cooled a little. Slow, so slow that she felt rather ridiculous, she drew the bra straps down her arms. At the same time, she held the cups against her breasts so only the upper mounds showed. Given what she'd hoped would happen today, she didn't know why she'd put on the stupid garment.

"I always buy the same brand of bra," she babbled. "You're a man so you probably don't know this, but finding one that truly fits isn't easy. Ah, this brand is pretty conservative but—"

"Shut up."

Sudden laugher bubbled up inside her and relieved a little of her tension. "You're right. It doesn't matter." *Only we do.*

She turned away from him, then back again, legs spread and her free hand dangling near her pubic hair—or it would have if it wasn't for the shorts. When his gaze shifted to her crotch, she ripped off the bra with a flourish and tossed it at him. It struck his chest. Before it could fall to the ground, he caught it. He wadded it into a ball, held it to his nose and inhaled, then dropped it at her feet.

If this was a real strip joint, she'd have on pasties, wouldn't she? Pasties and a g-string so the men could tuck bills there. Well, she had neither of those things, but she had put on black bikini panties this morning. As for why—

Weaker than she'd been back then—a hell of a lot weaker if truth be known—she fumbled at the snap on the waistband of her shorts. It resisted her tugging—either that or she couldn't concentrate—and she barely remembered to keep up her amateur bump and grind. The urge to laugh again bubbled through her. She killed it by concentrating on her physical response to what she was doing. She felt heavy between her legs, leaden and wet. *Ravenous.*

To stave off starvation, she ran through her memory of the night at the strip joint. Some of the girls had danced around poles that obviously represented giant cocks. They'd all but made love to those poles, sliding up and down them, rubbing various body parts over the sleek, hard surfaces. They'd kept their mouths parted and pouty. Their tongues had darted in and out, and their eyes couldn't be called anything except bedroom eyes. Although she hadn't admitted it to her friends, she'd been turned on by the dancers, maybe not as much as the men, some of whom had jerked off in public, but more than she'd expected.

She could get into this. Add to her income by moonlighting as a stripper. *No you can't. Only one man matters.*

Finally! Stifling the impulse to give herself a pat on the back, she turned her attention to the front zipper which fortunately didn't give her near the trouble the snap had. She unzipped it all the way, pushed a forefinger under the crotch of her panties and against her swollen lips, then pulled her shorts halfway back up. She thrust her pelvis at him. Laird's eyes remained riveted on her. Only his right hand moved—to cradle and further lift his swollen cock.

Yes, she'd gotten to him, no doubt about that.

Nearly as much as he'd gotten to her.

Her cheeks felt flushed and there was a crawly sensation from throat to the back of her neck. She couldn't swallow. It was all she could do not to start playing with herself in desperate determination to end this burning need. What had begun as a half-assed attempt to entice Laird had snared her.

The second time she pulled the zipper tab down, she let it stay that way and turned her attention to pushing the denim off her hips. She felt trapped by it and had to fight the need to rip and tear. She remembered—just barely—to keep it slow. At length the garment slid down her legs and, after kicking off her shoes, she stepped out of her shorts. She was exposed, nearly. Naked, nearly. Certainly there was no turning back, maybe ever.

Did she really know what she was doing? Would she survive?

It didn't matter.

Feeling a bit like a cowboy preparing for a gunfight, she hooked her thumbs over what there was of her panties. She slid them from side to side, the friction adding to her arousal.

The plan? What had the damn plan been?

Didn't matter.

After rolling the panties down as far as she could but not stepping out of them, she again clamped a hand over her crotch and worked her forefinger into her and against her aching bud. Her mouth wouldn't close. She stared at Laird but couldn't make him come into focus.

He stepped toward her.

She stumbled, closed the distance between them.

He reached for her, but at the last instant, she sidestepped him. Releasing herself, she took possession of his cock and either dropped to her knees or collapsed. Truth was, she didn't remember planning this in advance. Mouth open, not believing how lustful she felt, she looked up at him. He didn't move, gazed at her through hooded eyes, waited for her.

No more waiting.

Leaning toward him, she licked the head of his shaft. A drop of semen was already there. Capturing it, she pulled it into her mouth. Another drop instantly formed, and she kept her attention fixed on his great, commanding cock, even now only half comprehending that he was letting her do this to him. Last time he'd been the one in control, the one doing. Quite possibly he still held the balance of power.

It didn't matter.

Nothing escaped her wet tongue. She laved the opening slit, pressed the tip of her tongue into it and tasted his sweet, salty come. She couldn't believe her boldness or how erotic the act. Almost before she knew it was happening, an intense shudder shook her. She tilted on the edge of a climax.

Go for it! Let it happen.

No, not yet. This is about him. Him!

She sucked in air, but instead of it calming her, she inhaled Laird's earthy scent. Refusing to touch herself, she pushed out with her pelvic muscles and panted, taking shallow breaths so his scent couldn't reach her again. After a hard and exhausting minute, her body merely hummed, no longer burning its way to explosion. Waiting. Content. For now.

Although she hadn't had nearly enough of tasting his come, she didn't trust herself to go back to doing that. Neither, however, could she make herself leave his cock. Living in the moment, she turned her attention to the corona, gliding over sensitive flesh until he gasped and grabbed a handful of her hair. Just like a man, he was ready to get down to business.

But not yet. Not yet.

Settling herself lower on her knees, she took his balls in one hand, his cock in the other. She tried counting sheep, remembering the names of all the states, even mentally designing her dream home. None of those distractions worked. Giving up and hoping that her commitment to keep him rooted in today's world would be enough to keep her under control, she gently drew on his scrotum until his balls retreated into his body, then let up on the pressure until they emerged. Control could be heady...not that she really knew since she couldn't stop her pelvis's rhythmic thrusts, the need to press her butt cheeks together.

To have him fill her.

A fresh droplet appeared at the tip of his penis, and she licked it away, then moistened her lips, opened her mouth even more and breathed a hot breath on him. His grip on her hair increased. The tension helped distract her from her just-out-of-reach climax, but it didn't hurt.

Looking up at him, she showed him her wet tongue and lips before licking the base of his shaft. Inch by inch, she worked her way up the rigid column, then ran her tongue around the sensitive underside of his head. He moaned, the sound low and primal. A twin groan escaped her.

No longer able to ignore her inflamed cunt, she released his balls and caught one of her nether lips between thumb and forefinger. Her clit slipped free of its sheath, and she turned her attention to it, teasing and touching. Groaning.

Half mad, she swung her tongue around and around his knob, lingering at the underside because it obviously gave him so much pleasure. He clamped his hands over the sides of her head, holding her in place, pressing his cock against her lips. For a moment—only a moment—she resisted his thrust. Then, with her forefinger deep inside her cunt and curving forward toward her aching clit, she drew his cock into her, and closed her lips around the knob. She sucked gently, moistened him with her saliva, and tilted her head so she could accommodate perhaps half his length. Her forefinger danced between the lips of her cunt. Her nail feathered her clit, causing her to sob deep in her throat.

Her pelvis, beyond her control, drove toward him, begging him to somehow complete what she was doing to herself. She was aware of nothing except his size inside her mouth, filling her. No longer gave a damn about making it last.

He began an urgent and disjointed thrust and retreat, thrust and retreat. Somehow she kept pace, sliding her lips back up to the tip of his cock and flicking her tongue against it. She twisted her head from side to side, up and down, around and around. She sucked—sometimes gently, sometimes hard.

His cock touched the back of her throat, half gagging her and driving her insane at the same time. She swallowed, briefly catching and trapping him.

He again grabbed twin handfuls of her hair and forced her face even closer to him. His muff tickled her nose, adding to her pleasure. He pierced her throat over and over again, grunted and fought for breath. She repeatedly flicked her clit, duplicating his thrusts. Even with him deep in her, she moaned, moaned again.

His powerful hips pounded away, grinding and jerking. She danced to his rhythm, found one of her own, and melted the two together. The Everglades hissed and hummed, steamy heat rose around her. She felt herself diving into the heat, didn't give a damn how much came from her surroundings and how much she was responsible for.

Fighting off her climax earlier had been exhausting, but she'd become strong again—a marathoner heading for Olympic gold.

Let it rip! Let it come.

It didn't matter which of them broke out in a sweat first, who had the first climax, even who lasted the longest.

Higher. Even higher. To the mountaintop. Standing on it, arms flung wide and accomplishment hurtling through her.

Done.

Done and begun.

Someone was trying to get her attention, but she wanted to remain inside the fog and concentrate on her still-purring nerve endings. She'd never felt so weak—or satisfied. So encompassed by male sexuality. She was vaguely aware of aching jaws and a burning in her chest, probably from breathing so deep and fast.

"Mala?"

Laird! She'd know that voice anywhere.

"What?" Her throat felt raw and she tasted his come.

"Too fast."

"What—no it wasn't," she protested, although her plan had been to slowly drive him crazy. To make him her sex slave. "It was perfect."

She'd collapsed onto her haunches following her climax and was now curled up in something approaching a fetal position. Somehow her underwear had wound up around her ankles, and she felt hog tied. Eventually she'd have to do something about it. He'd knelt beside her and was massaging the back of her neck. From his glazed expression, she guessed he wasn't thinking about what he was doing. Just the same, the tender gesture brought her to tears.

"Nothing like this has ever happened to me," she started, then wound up laughing. "No kidding. I'd dare say it's new for you too. Maybe not the sex, but why we're here."

She turned so she could study his features. He'd stopped massaging her neck and remained on his knees scant inches away. Strangely, she felt as if she'd known him forever, yet had never seen him before. One thing: her half-assed plan to control him through sex had backfired. Royally. "Have you ever fucked in the Everglades?"

"It does not matter."

She wanted to believe that, to agree with him and not have to think about the women who'd come before and why he'd changed everything about her, but she couldn't.

"I nearly got married last year," she told him.

"Why did you not?"

"A lot of reasons. We'd been going together for a couple of years and when he asked me...he was kind, considerate. Brought me flowers and always wanted to know what I wanted, you know, in bed."

"Why did you not marry him?"

The answer was beyond complex and yet unbelievably simple. She ran her fingers over Laird's chest, not stopping until she was halfway down his flat belly. She wanted to claw at his belly until she found her way inside, wanted his blood to run over her fingers.

"Because we never fucked." She laughed again, delighted that she could say the word. "We had sex. He called it making love, so I guess that's what it was. In bed with the lights out. Sometimes soft music on the stereo and sometimes with wine on the nightstand."

She absently—or maybe not too absently—massaged first one of his hip bones and then the other. If anyone asked, she'd say yes, she was content to spend the rest of the day sitting here looking at Laird's naked body. Touching him.

"You and I have not fucked," he said.

That caught her attention. From the first time she'd seen him, she'd thought of precious little else, but he was right. Despite all the liberties he'd taken with her, and she with him, his cock had yet to bury itself inside her.

She didn't know how he felt about her masturbating and didn't feel bold enough to ask him. Maybe he believed that the only way a woman could, or should, satisfy herself was with a man's cock buried in her. But she'd wanted to do everything possible to make his climax memorable. She thought she'd accomplished that. There was nothing wrong with getting a little pleasure out of it herself—more than a little, if truth be told.

With her memories swirling around her, she stretched out on her side, propped herself up on an elbow, and regarded him. After a few seconds, he did the same so they were reclining face to face, nude bodies inches from each other. He used the hand not engaged in supporting his powerful body to lift her slightly drooping breasts.

"A woman's breasts," he said from low in his throat. "Full."

"I can't argue with that." Much as she enjoyed having him explore her, now that sanity had returned, she acknowledged that she'd come for much more than sex. "What's it like? Being where you are now, what does it feel like?"

"I am learning. I know they are my people. For the first time in my life, I have a family. But I am a stranger to their world."

He'd been speaking in that distinctive way again, as if English wasn't his native language. Determined to keep the commitment she'd made to return him to the only world he'd known, she rolled toward him. He met her halfway, his lips parted. She opened her mouth and sealed the contact.

It was, she realized, their first true kiss. Tears filled her throat. Desire stirred inside her, and yet it went deeper than lust. If she wasn't careful, she might fall in love with him and love, with his world turned on end and hers ruled by passion, could shatter her. Later, please, when all this was behind them, they'd talk about where their relationship was going and what each of them was capable of bringing to it—at least she hoped they could.

Determined not to lose sight of that hard reality, she

nonetheless ran her tongue over his teeth before nibbling on his lower lip. His hold on her breast tightened.

Without warning, her supporting left arm went numb, forcing her to roll onto her back. She flexed her elbow. "Old age catching up to me," she admitted. "Either that or I weigh more than I used to."

"Your weight is perfect." He demonstrated his approval by scrunching closer and spanning both her breasts with one large hand. As he drew them together, she glanced at his cock. So much for having spent himself a few minutes before. She slid her hand under the swollen shaft and supported it and his balls as best she could.

"So is yours," she whispered.

He chuckled. The sound made her wonder what it would take to have that laughter freely given. His laughter felt like a gift, something she'd cherish forever.

"Have you ever been to Disney World?" she asked despite the distraction of what she held and was beginning to feel again. Discovering his layers was vital. "Living here in Florida, maybe when you were a child—"

"No."

She swallowed back tears. "That says so much, doesn't it? A boy no one thought to take to Disney World."

"It does not matter."

Yes it does! And soon, somehow, some way, they'd go there.

"What you need is a second childhood—a real first one, that is," she told him with his manhood safely in her grasp. "Only you don't feel like a child to me today."

"I am not. And neither are you."

Hopefully there'd be time for more conversation, but not now. Turning her attention to his balls, she squeezed them together. He responded by sitting up, straddling her, and supporting his weight on his knees which improved his access to her and freed his hands. His fingers tiptoed over her belly, lightly brushing her navel until she swore the sensation went clear through her.

"You're ready for this?" she managed.

"Are you?"

She gave him her answer by shifting her hold on his cock, spreading her fingers as far apart as they'd go so she cradled his entire length. Doing so gave her an intense sensation of power. At the same time, she felt a little the way she had once when a hurricane had come dangerously close to where she lived before veering away.

Almost before it registered, he'd slid his hands under the back of her knees, drawing them first up and then out. Forced to release his penis, she grabbed his wrists and arched her back, increasing his access to her.

You're a mare in heat, aren't you? she asked herself.

So? Is there anything you'd rather do than get mounted?

No, she answered herself as he slipped his fingers through her muff, paused at the entrance to her pussy. Leaving her nether lips untouched, he pressed into the crease between legs and cunt and rubbed until she lifted her hips off the ground, begging him to fill her.

He ignored her, increased the torture by now repeatedly brushing his thumbnail over her cunt as if he was painting it. Staring at him, she noted that he was looking at her, bold and intense as if memorizing her core's contours. When she'd first become aware of the sensations the area between her legs was capable of, she'd been almost afraid of herself. Even now, even when she played with herself, she almost never looked at her sex organs.

Because she'd been repressed or afraid of herself before he'd come into her life?

Almost as if he'd heard her thoughts, he touched her wet opening, floated away, touched and again retreated. She swore she could feel her clit slide past its sheath. She dripped, dampening his fingers. Her clit was so heavy, so hot. Incredible!

"Laird, please!"

"Already?"

"Yes! Yes."

Using his wet fingers, he opened her outer lips. Much as she wanted to watch what he was doing, she had to be satisfied with her imagination. Her sex would be rose-tone, maybe red. In contrast, his fingers were dark. Her flesh was soft and smooth, pliant when he was all hardness and control.

Control? God yes!

Her fingers dug into his thighs as he gently, so gently, played with her inner lips. Once, twice, maybe three times he touched her clit. Each feathered brush drove her half out of her mind. Her clit danced under his direction.

He dove and retreated, spread his fingers slightly, plunged even farther. Small firecrackers exploded inside her.

Heaven!

But not, damn it, not the real thing!

So? What does it matter? He likes what he's doing. You sure as hell do.

I want to fuck him! Damn it, I need to be fucked!

"No!" she gasped. On the brink of a climax, she squeezed her legs together, immobilizing his fingers between her trembling thighs. "No. Not—that—way," she insisted when he tried to pull free. *Laird, please.*

Chapter Ten

"I want to do this for you," Mala told Laird. "It isn't about me."

"It was a minute ago."

"I know," she admitted. Damn, talking was hard. If only she wasn't so hot and bothered and the mental argument she'd just had with herself hadn't taken so much out of her. "I shouldn't have let that happen." She focused on breathing. It didn't help much, but it was better than nothing. She couldn't begin to direct the words tumbling out of her. "I can't begin to understand what you've been through, the responsibilities they want you to assume. A week ago you knew nothing about your heritage. Now it's become everything, or at least they'd want it to be."

He'd stopped walking his fingers over her belly and had rocked back on his haunches to regard her. Sunlight and shadows played across his features and naked body. He no longer seemed real—a spirit or ghost, maybe.

"I don't understand what's happening," she continued. She made no attempt to sit up but that didn't stop her from running her hands up and down his rock-like thighs. In another time and place, there'd be nothing except their bodies speaking to each other until they'd been rendered deaf or died in the attempt. "I'm not sure I ever will. But that's not important."

He cocked his head to one side. She couldn't tell what he was thinking.

"Laird, you don't dare lose contact with the world that's been your reality up until this point. That's why I came back." She slid her fingers around to the insides of his thighs. "To make sure you don't forget what's always sustained you." *To bring you back with me.*

"It does not matter." He placed his hands over hers but didn't try to stop her exploration.

"Yes, it does." This wasn't the time for conversation. "Laird, I want to be on top. Do things to you, be in control, instead of the way it's been between us so far."

He stared at her still-exposed cunt. "You did not like it?"

"I loved it," she admitted. He'd see through her lie if she told him anything else. "But bringing myself to climax because you weren't in a position to do it—a certain something was lacking. And just now, you wanted to play with me the way I'd done with you. It felt—wonderful. But it's not the same as sex the old-fashioned way. Something—was missing." At the moment, she couldn't think what that something might be, but he didn't need to know how good her earlier explosion had felt.

Without explaining what she had in mind, she slid out from under him and sat up. Before today, no matter who she'd gone to bed with, she'd always been aware of being naked and the sense of vulnerability that went with it. Now, however, wearing nothing felt more right than it ever had. She wasn't particularly proud of her body. It was all right, she guessed, particularly her large breasts, but a lifetime of wearing clothes had left her uneasy with the alternative. At least it had until now.

After checking to make sure the ground was covered with a soft carpet of vegetation, she took hold of Laird's shoulders and pressed against them. He gave her a quizzical look, then allowed her to position him on his back with his legs together. His erection saluted her. Not making any effort to hide her excitement, she straddled his legs. When he reached for her hips, she pushed his hands away and placed them at his waist. She couldn't take her eyes off his swollen cock, could barely think beyond the throbbing in her cunt. She smelled, not just her own excitement, but his sun-drying come.

Guided by instinct and need, she leaned forward and kissed the tip of his penis. The gesture felt both familiar and new—exciting. Her breasts dangled over him, the nipples puckered and so hard it was almost painful. Moisture pooled at her pussy, and a single drop broke free to run down the inside of her leg. Dispensing with preliminaries, she positioned herself over his cock, reached between her legs to spread her wet lips and slowly, easily slid him inside her.

He fit. Belonged. Filled her.

"There," she moaned.

"There," he repeated.

With her hands resting on his chest, she settled herself over and around him, sealing the connection. She'd been intent on his response and making sure he understood that this time she called the shots. As a result, she wasn't ready for the unbelievable sensation of having him inside her. This was sex, pure and simple. Primitive and elemental!

His cock twitched inside her, then seemed to expand even more until it filled her being. She might never be free again.

Gasping, she threw her head back and sucked in as much air as her lungs could hold. She'd taken one breath and was reaching for another when she felt him grasp her hanging breasts and pull her close. Not sure why, maybe because she felt as if she was on a roller coaster ride, she leaned away from him. He held on, clamping down on her breasts until they burned. She tried to meet his eyes, but her vision had blurred.

Over and over again, he lifted his pelvis off the ground, the thrust and rhythm vibrating deep in her. She swore she could taste him. Not content to let him do all the work, she rode him as if he were a stallion.

It didn't matter that their timing was off. No matter what he did, she adjusted herself to him, lost herself in his force. A mare might stand straddle-legged while a stallion plunged into her, but she refused to act like a dumb animal. She rocked, retreated and advanced, caught the last seat on the roller coaster and hung on with all her strength.

He plunged deeper and deeper inside her, his cock grinding against the sides of her throbbing cunt. Determined to keep him buried in her, she clamped her muscles around him, trapping him.

Control! This time I'm in control.

Yeah, sure!

He released her breasts and quickly clamped his hands over her rib cage and pushed. She couldn't be sure, but it felt as if he was trying to push her away from him, to free himself.

"No," she said. *No, you're mine.*

Giving weight to her thoughts, she ground her pelvis against his, her weight holding him in place. At the same time, she rocked back and forth, back and forth, taking his cock with her. She straightened somewhat and pressed the inside of her knees against his hips. She tried to slide her fingers between them so she could grip the base of his shaft, but the seal between them was complete, and there wasn't room. Undaunted, she again leaned forward and rested her forearms on his chest. He'd stopped trying to push her away, but his hands remained locked around her hip bones.

She rocked, pushed and pulled, sealed him inside her.

"Fuck me," she insisted. "Give it to me!"

He surged upward, nearly dislodging her.

"No! Damn it, give it to me."

Another surge followed by a quick retreat as if he was trying to suck her into him. Laughing, she slightly decreased her lock on him, allowing him the freedom to pump. He did so—again and again. Slammed his body against and into her. She laughed, nearly howled.

He came, came again, grunted and sweated. Dug his nails into the earth and used that to shove himself so deep inside her that she felt impaled. His sperm flooded her.

Riding the crest of his ejaculation, she leaned over and onto him. Pumped and pumped, pushed and retreated. Her clit quivered, shook, spasmed. She turned her head to the side and screamed.

Came.

Mala felt drenched in sweat. She couldn't remember where she left off and Laird began. They occupied two separate bodies. She knew that. But now she lay exhausted on top of him with his flaccid penis still tucked inside her. When finally she could put her mind and body to it, she tightened her pelvic muscles around him.

He looked up at her through sleepy eyes. "Not yet," he whispered. "In a few minutes—"

"I'll need more than that," she admitted. "I just—I just wanted to feel you in me."

"There is not much of me left."

"I don't care." On the verge of admitting how precious this union was, she held back. Years of playing the man/woman game should have taught her to be cautious, to not let her heart take command. Still, acknowledging how close she was to admitting he'd reached her heart frightened her.

"Laird?"

He blinked and focused on her, but she didn't speak until she'd slid off him and onto her knees—not because she wanted to but her weight pressed against his hip bones had to be uncomfortable.

"I met your brother. Did I tell you? Of course I did. I'm still—"

"He is not my brother."

"I know. But you think of him that way, don't you?"

He nodded. Although he looked half asleep, she plunged on. "He's the only family you have. He didn't tell me much. Just enough that I have some idea of your upbringing."

"Do you?"

Of course she didn't. The thought of never knowing what it meant to have parents brought her to the brink of tears.

"And I saw where you live—the place you built. You have a right to be proud of it."

He chuckled and flattened his hand over her rib cage. "I am not sure it would pass a building inspection."

"But it's yours." She forced her mind off his hand—tried to anyway. "Because a place to call your own is important to you."

He didn't say anything and had grown tense, wary. *Don't get too close,* she read. But if she didn't try, she'd always regret it.

"After all those years of being tossed from one foster home to another, finally, no one can force you to move again."

"Clint told you that?"

"No. I figured it out by myself." Made uneasy by his

tension, she sought to defuse it by feathering his cheeks with kisses. "Laird, I spent years working for someone else. I've been a cashier, a bank teller, a receptionist in a dentist's office. Those jobs paid the bills and most of the time I enjoyed the people I worked with, but nights and weekends were devoted to making jewelry."

"All your nights and weekends?" He ran his fingers down her belly and buried his nails in her pubic hair.

"No," she managed. She should be satiated, unconscious. Instead, his touch had awakened desire. "Not—not all of them."

"I did not think so."

She'd come back to the Everglades to try to get him to leave with her. She couldn't forget that, didn't dare.

"Don't," she warned and rolled away from him. She scrambled to her knees and made a feeble attempt at covering herself. Leaves and dried grasses stuck to her sweaty flesh. "If sex is the only thing between us, that's sad."

"Is it?"

"Yes," she insisted. "Your brother told me there've been a lot of women in your life."

"A few."

"How many do you remember? How many did you want to spend the rest of your life with?"

He sat up and regarded her. His nakedness obviously didn't bother him. Only, he wasn't completely naked because he wore the leather necklace. "What business of yours is it?" he challenged.

That stung, but she didn't allow herself to wallow in self-pity. "Will you answer something for me, Laird? If you hadn't reached out for me when all this began, who would it have been? Those women—would any of them have interrupted their lives for you? Can you even remember their names?"

His hands balled into fists. His glare seared through her. Fighting fear, she forced herself not to back down. "I don't want to pick a fight with you or make you defensive. That's the last thing I want."

Did she dare say more? Did she dare not? "The things you've done to me—I never knew it was possible," she admitted. "I—maybe I've waited my entire life for what's been happening."

"Have you?"

Although he sounded calm enough, she'd be a fool to allow herself to be sucked into his tone.

"Do one thing for me, please," she begged. "Before you turn your back on the only world you've ever known, the houseboat you built with your own hands, your business, return to it with me."

His expression darkened, putting her in mind of a trapped animal.

"Please." She looked around for her backpack, intending to show him the clothes she'd selected, but it wasn't there. Shivering, she scanned their surroundings but couldn't see anything of the Seminoles. Just the same, she had no doubt what had happened to the pack. The warning was clear. The Indians weren't releasing their hold on Laird. It occurred to her to let them have him and save herself from any more emotional upheaval, but she couldn't do that—for both their sakes.

Risking everything, she took his face in her hands and leaned forward until her mouth found his. He briefly returned her kiss, then turned away.

"They need me here," he said.

"But is it what *you* need? Is it?"

He didn't answer.

"Laird? You've been in here since the accident. They did that deliberately, are trying some kind of mind control. You can't let them get away with that. You can't!"

"They need—"

Not taking her eyes off him, she cradled his cock and balls and gently closed her fingers over them. "So do I," she whispered.

I know, she heard him say inside himself.

The farther they got from the Everglades, the more remote Laird became. Now that Alligator Alley was behind them, and they were nearing the marina where his business and house were, she counted herself lucky that she'd been able to convince him to put back on the loincloth before stepping out of the wilderness.

She'd turned the radio onto a sports talk station and even commented on how the local teams were doing, but he paid no attention. She'd kept her right hand near his thigh and had occasionally run her fingers over him in a subtle reminder of the sex they'd shared.

Fortunately, he hadn't insisted on driving, since he obviously wasn't concentrating on what was going on around him. She had no doubts his thoughts were on what he'd left behind, but there was no way she'd bring that up. Instead, she held on to the hope that familiar surroundings would snap him out of his lethargy—if that was what it was.

She'd hoped they could make it from the parking lot to the houseboat without anyone seeing them, but as they were navigating the floating walkway, an expensive pleasure boat glided past. The two men leaning against the railing stared and one's drink glass slipped out of his hand to fall into the water. Their female companions, making Mala think of trophy wives, first gaped at and then applauded Laird. He didn't appear to notice. Mindful of the fact she hadn't bothered with her bra when getting dressed, she folded her arms across her breasts.

When they reached his place, she reminded him they didn't have a key. How were they going to get in? His look made her wonder if her words were incomprehensible to him, but after a moment, he walked over to the heavy rope holding the houseboat in place and reached for something at the base of the anchoring post. With a key in his hand, he rejoined her. Then he unlocked the door and walked in, leaving her to follow after him.

He'd left a couple of windows open, but the compact interior smelled of stale air. Ignoring it and him, she took in her surroundings. Everything from the handmade coffee table with driftwood legs to a couch and chairs in browns and blues cried out "masculine". Three photographs of the bay—two at sunset and the other taken at dawn—constituted the only wall decorations. The kitchen was adjacent to the living room but divided from it by a waist-high counter and a couple of stools. A quick glance reinforced her suspicion that Laird didn't spend much time cooking, but at least the small refrigerator looked nearly new. She loved the exposed ceiling beams and round windows, the sense of wood and sea.

When she turned her attention to Laird, she realized he hadn't moved.

"What is it?" she asked.

He shrugged.

"Do you think someone's been here?"

Another shrug, this one reinforcing her fear that he had yet to reconnect with his life.

"You must be tired," she said. "And hungry. Do you want me to see if I can pull together something for you to eat?"

This time he didn't acknowledge that she'd spoken. He was looking out the window that faced the open sea.

"Do you want to go there?" she asked. "We could get in one of your boats and—"

"No."

Getting something out of him should have encouraged her, but it didn't. She also knew not to press. He looked so lonely standing in the middle of what was probably the only place he'd ever called home. Unable to leave him like that, she came to stand behind him and wrapped her arms around his waist. Feeling his legs against hers brought desire rushing back. She pressed herself closer, but he didn't respond.

Don't close me out, please. But maybe he had no control over his mood.

She sucked in what she hoped would be a calming breath, then wrinkled her nose. "You need a shower," she whispered into his ear. *We both do.*

Unfortunately, there was no "both" in the travel-trailer sized shower. However, because there was only a shower curtain, she pushed it aside and soaped him as he stood naked and remote under the spray. She loved the way the water ran down his finely honed body, particularly the small trickles curving toward his groin before disappearing under his dark pubic hair.

Once she'd scrubbed his upper body with the faded washcloth, lingering over each bone and muscle, she turned her attention to his lower half. By then she was nearly as soaked as he was. Inch by inch, she ran the washcloth closer to his penis. She turned the act into a game, teasing and retreating, barely touching, then pressing the flesh on the inside of his thighs. Little by little his cock responded. When he was fully erect, she folded the cloth over his shaft like a mother swaddling her baby in a receiving blanket and massaged.

He stared at nothing.

Frustrated and closer to tears than she cared to admit, she unwrapped and dropped the cloth and replaced it with her fingers. The sensation of hard, soap-slickened skin made her wild to tear off her sodden shorts and squeeze in beside him—at least it did until he grabbed her wrists and pushed her away from him. Without so much as a word of explanation, he turned his back on her and reached for the shampoo.

Hugging herself, she watched him. Shampoo foam slid down his broad back, briefly pooled at the top of his hips, then ran down his buttocks. She swallowed, hard.

She had gotten to him. He wouldn't have had an erection or pulled her hands off his cock if she hadn't. If she tried a little harder, came up with something inventive—

When he ducked his head under the spray to rinse off the shampoo, her attention snagged on the sodden leather pouch dangling from his neck. He wasn't naked after all, was he? He hadn't left the past behind, not really.

When he straightened again, she thought he'd turn off the water, but he went back to resembling a mannequin. Much as she'd love to study him, she didn't dare—not until she'd ripped him free of the Everglades prison. Reaching past him, she stopped the flow. Then because she'd anticipated that that wouldn't make an impact, she handed him a towel.

"Start with your face," she told him. "But get out first."

He did as she prompted. Once he'd dried his face, she grabbed another towel and used it on his hair. She had to stand on tiptoe to accomplish the task and if her breasts wound up flattened against his chest, so be it. She wasn't sure whether she was relieved or disappointed when he made no move to touch her.

This wasn't about her and her tender ego. He wasn't pushing her away so much as struggling to find his place in the world. And if he chose the past?

What about her?

He'd dried his neck and shoulders without her having to spell out the procedure, but after that he must have lost interest in the task. Instead, he stared at his reflection in the mirror. Once, when her father broke his right hand, she'd shaved him. By the time the cast came off, she'd considered herself an expert—a skill a few men had complimented her on. She'd demonstrate her handiwork to Laird as soon as she—

Sudden anger, or maybe it was fear of the question she'd just asked herself, distracted her from her musing. Almost before she knew what she was going to do, she grabbed the shell-covered pouch and pulled on it, looking for the knot. She'd no sooner found it and was trying to figure out how to deal with wet leather than Laird clamped his hands over her shoulders. Growling, he shoved. She flew backward and crashed into a wall.

"What—" she gasped.

Before she could get another word out, he came at her. She tried to dodge out of his way, but it was impossible given the confined space.

"Laird, stop it!" she gasped as he pinned her to the wall.

"Do—not—touch—"

"I didn't mean—I'm sorry. I won't."

Breathing so rapidly she thought he might hyperventilate, he continued to lean into her while spearing her with a hate-filled look. She wasn't sure he recognized her. She certainly didn't know the creature he'd become.

"I wasn't going to throw it away." Try as she might, she only partly succeeded in controlling her panic. Her shoulders had gone numb from the pressure he was exerting on them. She couldn't move if her life depended on it. "I just—I couldn't think of any other way of getting through to you."

He shook his head. His parted lips and strong white teeth both fascinated and frightened her. Everything about him felt huge.

"It has power over you," she said as soothingly as possible. "I—you left the Everglades, but you brought part of it with you."

He shuddered and looked haunted. "A gift. Gift and responsibility."

Although she wasn't sure what he was talking about, now wasn't the time to ask for an explanation. At least he spoke. Maybe that meant she was getting through to him. She'd do whatever it took to reach him and get him to tell her what was going on inside him. He frightened her, and yet she sensed that his emotions were even more intense. The small bathroom seemed to have shrunk. He was everywhere, everything. And there was nothing civilized about him. Not that she wanted it otherwise.

"I-I realize that," she managed. He was using his legs to pin her against the wall. As a result, his cock was being driven into her belly. Did she dare take hold of it, try to distract him? No matter. She couldn't move her numb arms. "Laird? You're hurting me."

He leaned away but didn't free her. His gaze raked over her, then settled on her breasts under the wet fabric. Her already hard nipples became even more so. For some insane reason, her attention locked on the drip-drip-drip coming from the shower. She was glad the mirror was steamy because that way she didn't have to see her expression. Caught in the rhythm of dripping water, she was slow to sense the shifting of his muscles. By the time she realized what he was doing, it was too late.

One moment she was standing face-to-face with Laird. The next, he'd grabbed her around the waist and hoisted her over his shoulder. He whirled and headed out of the room, forcing her to press her head against his back to keep from hitting it on the door jam. Three long, determined strides took him from bathroom to bedroom. He again clamped his hands around her waist, this time pulling her off his shoulder and throwing her onto the bed.

Bouncing on the mattress, she stared up at him. No matter how hard she tried, she couldn't find anything she recognized in his features. They'd darkened, his eyes more animal than human, muscles as tense as a panther stalking prey.

"Laird! Laird, what are you—"

He grabbed her waistband, unfastening it and yanking down the zipper. A single rough tug had the garment off her. She was still trying to decide what to do if he started tearing at her top when he jerked off her shoes and panties. Then he sat beside her, his greater weight pulling her toward him. She was still afraid of him, unnerved and unsure. However, there was no denying that his rough treatment had also turned her on.

The need to let him know that must be responsible for the way her now tingling fingers reached for him. Finding his belly, she trailed her nails over his navel. She couldn't quite talk herself into meeting his eyes.

"It's all right, Laird," she said as soothingly as possible. "You've been through so much. It's going to take time to put it all behind you. I can—I know how to help."

"My—my name is Thunder."

"Thunder." She barely got the word out.

For the third time in less than a minute, he wrapped his hands around her waist, now repositioning her on the bed so she was in the middle of it. When he was satisfied, he pried her hands off him and pinned them over her head. Caught between a million conflicting emotions, she struggled to free herself, but lacked the strength. All her gyrations accomplished were to twist her top around her middle. She felt imprisoned by it. He solved that by pushing it up and over her breasts. She should have put back on her bra, not that it would have made a difference—or stayed on very long.

Without so much as a by your leave—not that she expected it—he pressed the heel of his hand against her right breast, flattening and trapping it but not causing pain. At the same time, he reached across the space between her breasts and fingered-massaged the left one.

Don't move. Don't let him know he's gotten to you. Turning the warning into action, she pressed her hips against the bed and kept her legs clamped together. She wanted to believe he knew the difference between play and force, but he now called himself Thunder. Who knew what was acceptable behavior in that world? If he forced himself on her, if he even started, would she fight him?

The real question was, did she want to?

Quickly, so quickly she didn't know how it was possible, he released her hands and breasts, forced her legs apart and settled himself on his knees between them. She tried to sit up, but he pressed a hand against her belly, holding her down. A growl rumbled deep in his chest.

Somewhere between anger and helpless anticipation, she slapped his arm. It must not have registered because he now stared at the thatch of dark hair over her pelvic area. She felt her cunt fill with hot fluid, and her inner thighs heated. No, that wasn't the response of a woman about to be forced against her will.

Once again he acted before she could prepare for it. This time he slid his hands under her hips and lifted, forcing her to bend her knees. Damn him, she wasn't some hooker he could ride! Yes, her pussy leaked and he'd have to be a fool not to know what that meant, but she was sick and tired of being manipulated. The truth was, she was scared.

Belatedly realizing she was lying there spread-eagle and gripping the bottom sheet, she tried to draw her knees together. He immediately pushed down on their insides and held her in place. She tried to lift one foot—what for she wasn't sure—but couldn't maintain the position. She whipped her head from side to side. His grip on her knees didn't let up.

"Don't! I don't—"

He bucked toward her and rammed the head of his cock against her cunt. Silenced, she stopped fighting the pressure on her legs. Her head fell back, her eyes closed, and she thought of nothing, felt nothing except him against her, determined shaft spreading her outer lips, gliding into her lubricated opening.

He filled her. Became part of her.

No you don't! You might be stronger than me, determined, but I will not, will not... He'd slipped inside her and become part of her. His cock plunged so deep inside that she felt him in her belly. With each thrust, he nearly slid out, paused at her aching clit, rubbed against it, turned flame into conflagration.

Don't! Don't let him...

Why the hell not? It's what you want.

She rode his thrusts with him, cried out in time with his grunts, felt herself climbing higher and higher, ever hotter.

"Thunder! Thunder, Thunder, Thunder!" she screamed.

Then she exploded.

She barely felt his mouth on the side of her neck, wasn't sure she'd actually heard him whisper, "I'm sorry."

Chapter Eleven

"Damn you. You did what you wanted, didn't ask how I felt—"

"You got what you wanted."

"That's not the point!" Mala shot back, even though he was right. "Just because you're turned on doesn't give you the right to—to jump on me."

"You didn't tell me to stop."

"I tried to. Besides, would it have made any difference?"

When Laird didn't say anything, she sat up and slid off the bed. Not bothering to look back at him, she walked into the bathroom and turned on the shower. She had no idea what she'd do if he came in after her, but he didn't, which left her to deal with questions. It would have been easier if the only thing she'd had to contend with was trying to figure out him and his actions, but there was also the undeniable issue of what the hell she was doing.

Laird had had his way with her. Humped her. If one looked at their last coupling from a purely cause-and-effect standpoint, that's exactly what had happened. However, it hadn't been rape. In fact it had been far from it.

Yeah, she amended as she scrubbed at her scalp, it had hardly been that. Rape meant to force one's will upon another, and he certainly hadn't had to force anything—because she'd wanted sex as much as he did.

Well, why wouldn't she? He was a stud, after all. More than a stud—the most complex and fascinating and overwhelming man she'd ever known.

In the middle of that admission, she touched the side of her neck. *"I'm sorry."* His whispered confession wrapped itself around her and brought her to tears. Why hadn't she seen it before? He wasn't fighting her, wasn't determined to impress her with his control.

He'd run his lips over her throat in a gentle, maybe loving gesture. No matter what was going on inside him, he cared about her. That care and compassion and his maybe desperate need to hold on to some piece of what he'd once been warred with recent changes. He didn't know how to tell her this. All he could do was kiss her in the moment of climax.

If only she had some idea what the future would bring or whether the past would suck him into it.

If he went back in time, and she couldn't follow him there anymore, how would she survive?

"I'm sorry," she told him later as they were eating the meal she'd thrown together from the few things she'd found in his refrigerator. They were sitting outside in the bolted down lawn chairs watching night steal over the sky. A stiff breeze tugged at their hair. She didn't care what hers looked like, and his windblown appearance only added to his appeal. She couldn't make herself believe he didn't know how sexy he looked, but she wasn't about to admit how turned on she'd become from just looking at his silhouette.

As far as she could remember, it was the first time they'd

simply sat in each other's presence. She prayed it wouldn't be the last and that she could tell him how grateful she was because he'd entrusted her with his gentle side, no matter how briefly. "I shouldn't have touched your necklace." Even now, it drew her attention.

He nodded, but continued to study the horizon, his silence reinforcing how little he'd spoken since leaving the Everglades. "I thought—I hoped that not wearing it would decrease its influence over you."

"It belongs with me."

"I understand that. Believe me, I do." *But that doesn't stop me from being afraid of what that means.* She balanced her plate on her knees and reached over to take his hand. Her heart felt as if it had caught in her throat, making it hard to talk.

"Laird, I want us to spend the night at my place."

"You do not like this?" He indicated the gently lapping water.

"I love it. But now that I've seen where you live, I want you to experience the same thing."

She wasn't sure what impact, if any, her words had made on him because now he was looking at her hand. On her forefinger was a ring she'd made from threads of silver braided together. She'd woven tiny white shells into the braid.

"You made this?" he asked.

"Yes."

"It is beautiful. The work of a true artist."

For the second time in less than an hour she was on the brink of tears. "You mean that?" she managed.

"You mean a great deal to me," he whispered. "I understand what is important to you, at least some things."

Speechless, she stared at him, but he didn't meet her gaze.

"I—I need to hear that," she admitted.

Instead of saying anything, he reached out and caressed her neck where his mouth had briefly rested.

Shaking, she pulled off her ring and slid it onto his baby finger. "I want you to have it."

He wiggled his fingers until the dying sunlight glinted off the silver.

"That's what I'd like you to see," she hurried on, glad to have a reason, any reason, to get him into her domain. To build on the connection, openness, and understanding they'd begun. "I have my studio there as well as the pieces I haven't sold or placed in stores. Maybe you don't care. A lot of men, well, they don't understand how much satisfaction I get out of creating jewelry."

"But it's important to you that I do?"

"Yes, it is." *Maybe it'll help keep you here.*

They left after dark and, although she would have let him if he'd offered to drive, Laird still showed no interest in getting behind the wheel. He'd needed her to remind him to bring along personal items and a change of clothing. What she didn't bring up was what they were going to do tomorrow or the things they might say to each other. In the back of her mind was the hope she could get him to talk to his brother and thus continue the transition back to the real world, but the only thing she was sure of was that she had to take it only one step at a time.

As she drove, she asked about his boating business, but because his answers were so brief, all she really understood was that he'd started by offering to taking people to his favorite fishing spots. As word of his success grew, the transition from hobby to business began. He loved spending his days watching the multitude of sea birds and creatures that lived in the shallow waters. He was less enthralled with some of his customers and considered boat maintenance a chore better done without thinking about it too much. Some day he'd like to have a sailboat but didn't regret spending money on a motorcycle instead. When she reminded him that neither of them had seen the motorcycle since the crash, he shrugged.

By the time she reached her small, older place inland, she'd run out of things to talk about related to how he made a living. She thanked him for his honesty and been rewarded with a small smile. Hoping he cared, she explained that thanks to a small inheritance from a grandfather, she'd been able to make a down payment on what had been a mother-in-law cottage behind a larger house until the previous owners had succeeded in getting a zone change. The cottage consisted of two bedrooms and a single bathroom in addition to a small living room with one wall that was all windows. She'd wanted it because the garage had been converted into a workshop.

After a cursory tour of the house, she took him into her workshop with its multitude of plastic containers filled with the shells she'd collected while walking the beaches, engraving tools, casts, soldering equipment, buffs, pliers, and carving tools, to say nothing of semi-precious stones. He looked both at home and like a stranger in her domain. To her surprise and gratitude, he asked how she created her work.

"It's in my head," she explained. "I don't always know it's there until I start looking at various materials and playing at ways to put them together. Like the ring you're wearing." She indicated it, but with her awareness of him in the crowded space on high alert, she didn't touch him. "I was watching some children playing a few weeks ago and noticed this blond girl with the longest, neatest braids. I wanted to duplicate that."

He stared at a tray filled with feathers while she struggled with the notion that he was too large and wild for the confined space. "What's that?" he asked, pointing at a long, lacy white feather.

"It's from a snowy egret. I got permission to scrounge what I could find at the wildlife rehabilitation center. Many years ago, the demand for egret feathers to decorate women's hats nearly made the birds extinct. I occasionally incorporate one into a necklace, but they're pretty fragile."

"You could use imitation, plastic, maybe."

"It wouldn't speak to me." She looked up at him, her attention catching, as she knew it would, on the necklace he now wore on the outside of his faded T-shirt. The leather was dry, almost brittle. Whatever its original color, it had nearly been bleached white.

Suddenly, she was struck by one of the flashes of inspiration she'd long encouraged. Barely noticing that Laird was watching her, she grabbed one of the sheets of paper she kept in her studio and began sketching a bracelet that bore a striking resemblance to his necklace. She worked for maybe ten minutes, occasionally erasing and refining but always with the same basic goal. Finally she straightened and held the paper at arm's length.

"What do you think?" she asked.

He stepped to her side and studied the drawing. Their shoulders touched, testing her vow to keep her hands off him. She was so aware of him, super-charged. "That is it," he said at length.

"Do you like it?"

"Yes." He leaned toward her, shared his heat with her. Once again she had to struggle against tears.

"That means a great deal to me," she admitted.

"You are a remarkable woman," he said. "Talented in ways I did not expect. I'm still wrapping my mind around everything I'm learning about you."

She'd had her creations praised by some of the state's harshest critics, but no other praise meant as much as his simple approval. The bracelet she could hardly wait to get started on wouldn't be an exact duplicate of his. Rather, she envisioned a slimmer, lighter version. She intended to use soft, white leather as the base, but instead of fastening ordinary shells to it, she'd choose a variety of colors ranging from palest green to violet.

"Yours is masculine," she explained. *Just like you are.* "Mine will be feminine. And in the pouch—what about a small silver arrowhead?"

"Why that?"

She ran her fingers over the sketch. "The Seminole gave me the idea. I want to honor them."

Cupping his hand around her chin, he forced her to look up at him. Sexual heat radiated from him, but she fought its dangerous impact. Not only wasn't there room for sex in here, she was suddenly afraid of the loss of control that happened whenever he made his physical demands on her.

"What?" she asked when he only stared at her.

"I'm trying to decide," he said, "whether you would be of use to me in the Everglades. You would..." Releasing her chin, he trailed his fingers over her throat and down to her cleavage. His fingers were like fire, a flame that turned into wet heat between her legs.

"You would what?" she heard herself ask.

"I have needs." He possessively palmed her breast. "You would fulfill them."

"That's all?" she stammered. "You want a sex partner?"

Instead of answering, he flattened her breast against her ribcage. The pressure spread throughout her, but centered in her cunt. Robbed of breath, she tried to back away from his strength and dominance. His expression unreadable, he reached down and forced his free hand between her legs. She leaned away from him, but a wall stopped her retreat. Arms heavy and limp at her sides, she struggled to keep her eyes open, and her mouth closed. Her thoughts went no further than the hand covering her breast, the other now locked over her cunt.

"You are mine," he growled. "You will never forget that."

Because the air-conditioning in her place couldn't keep up with the worst of summer's heat, Mala had taken to sleeping on her back porch under a large ceiling fan. Once Laird had released her and stalked out of her studio, she'd panted her way back to self-control. She'd briefly entertained the notion that she should throw him out on his ear. After all, he had his nerve thinking of her as his possession. But, damn him, he was right! She couldn't fathom long, frustrating nights without him. Besides, he'd become someone she didn't believe he had any control over.

Once she'd reconciled herself to how much a part of her he'd become, she told him about the back porch option, then added that he could blow up a spare queen-size mattress she kept around for guests.

They were already on the porch sipping iced tea, not touching, not even that close. She'd put on a shift that ended at mid thigh, but although she wore panties, she hadn't bothered with a bra. Or maybe the truth was, only finding the real him again mattered.

She'd thought he'd be exhausted after the day he'd had. Although she hadn't been able to do anything about her awareness of him, she could barely keep her eyes open. But the more night enveloped them, the more restless he seemed. He'd sit for a few minutes, then stand and stalk barefoot from one end of the netting-encased porch to the other, looking for all the world like a trapped animal. His cut-off jeans and ragbag-ready shirt only made him appear more uncivilized.

"What is it?" she asked when he began yet another circuit.

"They need me."

Suddenly chilled, she pushed herself to her feet. In truth, all she wanted was to lie down and go to bed—with Laird beside, or inside, her. But his simple, inescapable comment made that impossible.

"Who?" she asked because she had no choice.

"My people."

His people. "H-how do you know? Maybe—it's been a long, exhausting day."

He pressed his hand to his chest. The gesture flattened the pouch against his throat. "I feel it—here."

She stood beside him and wound her arm around his waist. As she expected, that was all it took for her desire to return. Wrapped in with longing was the fear he might disappear.

"What does it feel like?" she managed.

"Warmth. And Osceola's tears."

Osceola, she remembered, had been the Seminole's bravest and most famous chief, but beyond that, she knew pathetically little about the man.

"You feel his tears?"

"He placed this around my neck." Laird fingered the

necklace.

He couldn't have! she wanted to scream. *He's been dead for decades.* "Did—did he say anything?"

"Soon he will no longer be able to lead. He has already felt the chains and bars of prison."

"But—"

"That imprisonment lasted only a few days before he was freed and became head war chief." Laird spoke unemotionally as if reading from a text. "He now hears the footsteps of the American troops even in his sleep. Soon he will have to meet with the enemy to negotiate for the freedom of one of his chiefs. He has no choice, but his freedom is at stake. He does not trust their general. He needs someone to take his place."

"He—he's chosen you?" She felt dizzy.

"Yes." Laird pulled free, then pressed his hands over his eyes. "I look at my chief and see an ill man."

My chief. She might not have been particularly interested in history, but she did remember that Osceola had been sick when an artist had come to the prison where he'd been placed and painted a portrait of the chief—and that Osceola had died shortly after posing.

"Laird? Do you believe he's alive right now?"

Laird straightened and stared at her. "Now and then are like a river to me. Sometimes it flows one way. Then I step into the Everglades and much changes, but the river still flows."

Although she wasn't sure she understood, she didn't ask for further clarification. After all, her own perception of reality had undergone a profound change.

"You can't go to him tonight," she insisted. The longer she kept him from the Everglades, the greater her chance of breaking the tie—maybe. "Tonight is for us."

She waited, hoping he'd take the hint, but he only continued to study her—or maybe he wasn't thinking of her at all. Wishing someone somewhere had developed guidelines for keeping a man from being sucked into the past, she took his hands and placed them at the sides of her neck.

"Can you feel my pulse?" she asked. "I'm alive. Real. So are you. You—when we were in my studio, you said I belonged to you."

"One of his wives was the descendant of a slave," Laird whispered. He gave no indication he'd heard her. "They had a daughter. One day Chechoter was captured by slave catchers and sold into slavery."

"Hush, hush," she muttered, although what Laird had just said sickened her. How horrible. "You can't return her to her parents."

"I feel Osceola's tears. A father's tears."

"So do I," she admitted. She drew his hands over her unrestrained breasts. "Laird, Osceola had—has women in his life. You deserve the same. Me. Make me yours tonight. Brand me."

Perhaps that made an impact on him, and maybe he was simply responding to her invitation to explore her. At any rate, he knelt, took hold of the hem of her shift and unceremoniously drew it over her head, leaving her naked except for the thin nylon panties. She shivered as a breeze from the fan teased her breasts and puckered her nipples. Although there was little chance anyone could see them, she felt a little uneasy being stripped while out in the open. Uneasy and intrigued by the possibilities.

Before she could suggest going inside, Laird turned her so her back was to him. His warm breath on her nape made her shudder. Ignoring her reaction, he ran his fingers under her panties. Although they already left her navel exposed, maybe he thought they were too modest because he deftly rolled them down to the apex of her legs.

"You..." She tried again. "You aren't much into foreplay tonight, are you?"

"You do not want this?" He cupped his hand over her crotch and pulled her roughly against him. His swollen cock pressed into her buttocks.

"Yes," she moaned. "Yes, I do, damn it."

If anything, the pressure over her cunt increased until it became almost painful. Needing distraction, she planted her hands over his imprisoning wrist and pulled. Instead of releasing her, however, he pushed up with his fingers, probing at her labia. Her cunt loosened, softened, readied itself for him.

"Stop it! You're hurting me."

"Is that it?" He relaxed his grip a little. "Or are you afraid to give yourself totally to me? Become mine?"

Even as she lost herself in the heated sensation of having her cunt trapped by him, she continued to pull on his wrist. "Too much," she sobbed. "I can't keep on top of what you're doing."

"I will remember that," he said, and released her. The sudden loss of pressure forced her to cry out and sag forward. She broke into a sweat, and a climax hummed just beyond her reach. She would have told him that and begged him to help her into and through it, but she was afraid. Afraid of her own body.

Just the same, she hoped he'd complete the stripping he'd begun a few seconds ago. Instead, he closed his right arm over her breasts and once again pulled her hard against him. Once he had her imprisoned, he slid his left hand under the nylon and over her crotch. As before, her response was instant. No way wouldn't he notice her flooded cunt.

Chuckling—or maybe growling—he worked his middle finger between her throbbing lips and deep inside. She couldn't tell whether he was being less possessive this time, thus keeping her from feeling trapped, or she'd simply become accustomed to his brand of foreplay. Lightheaded, she attempted to steady herself by reaching behind her and grasping his thighs. It helped. It also left her even more exposed to his exploration.

At his silent prompting, she widened her stance. Beyond caring about anything except the intimate search, she threw back her head so it rested against his collarbone and shut her eyes.

His woman, his possession.

His finger—his magical finger—curled so it now rubbed the so-sensitive front of her passage. He reached and stroked, danced right and stroked some more, tiptoed left to repeat the exquisite torture. Her consciousness narrowed until nothing of her existed beyond the charged channel.

She could barely breathe, would have fallen if he hadn't clamped her against him. She wished to hell he was as naked as she.

Didn't matter.

Already on fire, she felt the inner flame grow even hotter. Something shifted inside her, and it took a moment to realize he'd straightened his finger and was pushing it even further inside her. His finger wasn't large enough to completely fill her pussy. Otherwise, maybe she would have already come.

Already?

Damn, what had happened to her? A simple finger job and—

Oh God! His nail teasing her super-charged clit, igniting swollen flesh, bringing her—bringing her—

Climax was a breath away. One more grazing motion and—

No!

"What—what are you doing?" she sobbed. Frustration made her crazy. He'd withdrawn his finger, leaving her on the brink.

"A lesson, Mala," he said in an impersonal tone. "You took advantage of me earlier today, pulled me away from my people when I was too weak to know what you were doing."

Hating him, she pulled out of his grasp and whirled on him. Another push of wind slid over her naked flesh, and her clit continued to boil.

"So you decided to torture me?" she demanded. She couldn't stop trembling.

"Call it what you want."

"I don't give a damn about word games!" On the brink of telling him to get the hell out of her life, she glanced down. He had an erection. "Foreplay," she said. "And now that you've had your turn, it's mine."

"Is this a fight?"

"I don't know what it is. Damn it, Laird. You've turned my life upside down and inside out. You care about me. I know you do! At least you do when *they* let you. We're going somewhere neither of us has ever gone before. If you think I was taking advantage of you—I wasn't. I wasn't!"

"Then what was it?"

If she had the rest of her life, she wasn't sure she could answer him. All she knew for sure was that he'd deftly brought her to the brink of ecstasy only to rob her. Now, somehow, she'd make it her turn. Let him know what it felt like to be trapped and a prisoner of sexual need. Fight for the human being she knew he could be.

Putting thought into action, she strode toward him, unzipped his shorts and yanked them off. When she reached for his briefs, he captured her wrist. "Are you afraid?" she taunted. "No turnabout?"

"I may be afraid of certain things, but not of you."

"I'd never do anything to hurt you, Laird," she told him. "I'd like to believe the same of you, but you might not be able to help it."

"You think that?"

"You're on a journey—a journey with an end neither of us can anticipate. If I get in the way..."

"What if you get in the way?" he prompted.

"I don't want to go into that now. And I don't believe you do, either."

By way of answer, he lifted her captured hand, brought it to his mouth and kissed it. She nearly melted at the gesture and might have told him how much it meant to her if she'd been able to ignore the moist heat between her legs or the sense that he wasn't in complete control of himself.

After standing on tiptoe and kissing him full but briefly on the lips, she again turned her attention to his briefs. This time he let her finish disrobing him. She heard a radio playing in the distance and guessed they weren't the only ones in the neighborhood to take advantage of a summer evening.

Let them have their late barbeques, their lawn games. She had something much more important to accomplish.

When she turned him so his back was to the mattress, the dim porch light placed him in silhouette. No longer being able to clearly see him gave her the uneasy feeling that he might disappear. She had to take advantage of whatever time they had together.

Sexual frustration still made it impossible for her to completely disregard her body, but she concentrated on him to the best of her ability. She'd called his titillation of her foreplay. Well, that worked both ways.

Dispensing with preliminaries, she slid both hands under his cock. With her right, she cradled the turgid length. She cupped the other around his balls and pressed them together, rocking them back and forth against each other at the same time. He reached for her.

"No," she warned, although she ached with the need to feel his hands swarming over her. "I didn't stop you when you rammed your finger inside me. When you brought me to the brink only to rob me. I deserve the same."

The same and yet different, she amended because her full intention was to force a climax out of him, not that she thought he'd object. She stroked and kneaded, then crouched down and sucked the tip of his cock into her mouth. The moment she did, he thrust his pelvis at her. Although she hated to, she turned her head to the side, releasing him. He tried to lean away from her, but she still had hold of his balls.

Quick and sure, she again captured his cock. She slid her palm up and down its length, fantasizing about feeding it into her cunt. Instead, she let go of his balls and took the hard, dripping spear in both hands. She pressed and twisted, duplicating as best she could having him inside her.

Faster and faster she stroked. As she did, she squeezed and released her buttocks, squeezed again, further stimulating herself. He thrust and retreated, thrust and retreated, harder and harder.

Wild to bring him to climax, she exerted what she hoped was just the right amount of resistance. She'd nearly let him pull his cock free only to reestablish control by sliding her hand down to its base and squeezing down first with thumb and forefinger and then the rest of her fingers. Pinpricks of sensation hummed along her fingers, spread to her palms, over her wrists. Her nipples had become so swollen that they pulled her entire breasts upward. Juices had already leaked from her core and now ran down the insides of her thighs, the smell blended with their sweat, further filling the space with the heat of sex.

"Come," she muttered. "Come. Let go."

He did, his come spilling out of him and over her fingers.

She sobbed, bucked away from him and jammed her wet fingers deep inside her. Unmindful of her strong nails, she prodded and tickled, pressed, released, then pressed again. Her head felt as if it might explode. She took noisy, ragged breaths full of his scent.

Suddenly, he shoved her onto her back. Spreading her legs and pulling her fingers out of her at the same time, he then bent her knees and slipped a pillow under her hips. Through a watery film, she saw him lower his head toward her exposed and waiting cunt.

"Yes!" she gasped. "Please, yes!"

He briefly licked at the juice clinging to her inner thighs, but she was too far gone, too close to the brink for that.

"Now! Please! Damn it, please!"

Oh my! Oh my God! His tongue kissing her clit! Now his teeth rubbing the swollen and sensitive flesh, making her sob. Heat consumed her.

She'd already started to come when his tongue probed between her nether lips, pushed her clit deep inside, held it there.

She exploded.

Came again as he buried his warrior's tongue deep inside her core. *I belong to you! Don't—don't forget that. Please.*

As consciousness faded, she reached up and pressed her hand over his throat. She couldn't be sure, but she thought she heard him sigh. Felt tension seep out of him.

Chapter Twelve

Mala lay on her side under Laird's outstretched arm and leg. She'd fallen asleep almost immediately after they'd collapsed onto the mattress. At first she wasn't sure what had awakened her, then thought it might have turned too cool for them to comfortably sleep naked. Taking inventory of her skin, she found no cool spots. Neither was she in any discomfort from the weight of his limbs. Despite the darkness enveloping her, her thoughts settled on his earlier sigh. The soft and vulnerable sound had been a gift.

She was nearly back asleep when she again jerked awake. This time there was no doubt of the cause. Laird was talking in his sleep. Only, she didn't understand a word he was saying. He'd done that before, and she'd been able to get him to speak in English again. How had she accomplished that?

Smiling faintly, she pushed out her butt, making contact. She discovered he had an erection and turned so she now faced him. She lifted her knee and then lowered it, thinking to rub it over his penis. Before she could complete the act, his body tensed.

"Laird, it's all right," she soothed. "You just had a dream."

Suddenly, he sprang to his feet, and she hurried to do the same. He'd turned off the porch light when they went to bed and now stood in the dark, invisible except for the faintest shape and tension that boiled from him.

"What is it?" she asked. Why she was backing away instead of trying to embrace him, she couldn't say.

More words erupted from him. She hugged herself. He stalked from one end of the porch to another, then slammed his fist against the screening.

"Don't!" she warned. "You'll break—"

Whirling, he came at her. She tried to duck under his outstretched arms, but he caught her upper arms and violently shook her. Mindful of the neighbors, she forced herself not to cry out. Instead, she pummeled his chest. He clamped down, and her arms instantly turned numb.

"Don't. Please, you're hurting me."

He didn't hear. Either that or he didn't care. He continued to shake her.

"What—what have I—ow!" She gasped. She'd bitten her tongue.

More foreign words spewed from him. He stopped shaking her and was trying to pull her against him. Leery of what he might do, she tried to knee him in the balls. Unfortunately, her aim was off, causing her knee to glance off his thigh. Before she could try again, he lifted her half off her feet and threw her to the mattress.

Instead of coming after her, he charged the netting, ripped it apart, and jumped to the ground. She heard him run off.

Late afternoon found Mala in her shop. Although half sick from exhaustion, she'd known better than try to sleep. And now that she'd unsuccessfully tried to contact Laird's brother, driven over to the marina only to find his business and houseboat locked up, and conducted some research at the library, she was doing the one thing that might put her mind at peace.

After taking a sip of iced tea—the only thing she'd been able to put in her stomach—she focused on what she'd created. The bracelet was essentially the same as the drawing she'd shown Laird except she'd wound up using even smaller shells. She still had to fasten a clasp to it before it would stay on, but when she draped it over her wrist, she felt satisfied—or at least as satisfied as someone whose life was in turmoil could.

She'd left a message asking Clint to please get in touch if he heard from his "brother" and hadn't really expected to find Laird either at home or work. What truly upset her was what she'd learned from her research. Following Osceola's death, the Seminole had continued to hold out against the whites, but within three years, most had surrendered and been relocated west of the Mississippi.

A few holdouts had fled deep into the Everglades, apparently to live out their lives in the swamps. Nothing was known about their lives as fugitives, but some of their great-great-grandchildren continued to live much as the ancient Seminole had. Had they survived, endured, thrived, because they'd followed a brave and competent leader?

The bracelet started to slide off her wrist, and she held it in place. Despite her reliance on natural materials, she'd always taken pride in clean, smooth, lines—what one critic had called a refined polish. This piece looked as if it had been fashioned by someone unschooled in the craft. It was primitive and crude— like the necklace that had served as her inspiration.

She closed her eyes, but didn't try to hold back her tears. Wherever Laird was, she had no doubt he wore the necklace Osceola had given him.

Maybe all she'd ever have of her lover was this bracelet.

That and memories of the most intense and unforgettable sex of her life.

The warrior known as Thunder bent low to the ground. His rough and callused feet were silent as he slipped closer to the enemy. His senses were alert to the sights, sounds and smells of the Everglades, and he felt as one with his surroundings. Even his heart beat in time with his world. The sun had bronzed him. His muscles were hard. As before, he'd found something to wear and weapons on the path. Naked except for the loincloth, he felt the reassuring pressure of the knife at his side, the bow and arrows strapped to his back. He couldn't say how long he'd been walking or when and how he'd known he'd gotten near men who would kill him if they had the chance.

Seated deep inside him was knowledge of the men, women and children who made up his family. Their words of encouragement and confidence rang inside him and created their own rhythm.

And yet there was something else—a touch that didn't come from his people. A woman's slender but strong arms, her body blending with his. Again and again as he walked, she came to him, tried to take over his thoughts and body, fought to make him forget that the lives of the Seminole depended on his knowledge of the enemy.

Why would she try to come between him and his task? His destiny?

Why was her hold on him so strong?

Something—it might have been the woman's fingers—brushed his breast. He lifted his hand, intending to push her away. Instead, his gaze settled on the ring on his smallest finger. Stopping, he turned his hand one way and then another until a shaft of light from the dying sun struck it. He didn't recognize the material it was made from, and yet his head echoed with her explanation of how she'd woven silver strands together to duplicate a child's braid.

And he'd placed her creation on his finger.

A tentacle of fear raced through him, but when he grabbed the ring, he couldn't make himself tear it off and throw it away.

She had hold of him.

Had captured him.

No!

"Yes."

Heart pounding, determined to learn where her voice had come from, he stared at his surroundings. He didn't want to admit that she'd left her word inside him, maybe was speaking to him from a great distance, but perhaps he had no choice.

No! She would *not* control him!

Control belonged to him.

Mala jerked awake. She'd barely comprehended that she'd fallen asleep at her work bench when the full truth of what was happening struck her. No matter that she was alone with only the breeze from the overhead fan to keep her company, Laird had found her.

No, not Laird. Thunder.

Thunder, who understood her body better than she ever could.

She stood because she had no choice. Self-control had nothing to do with walking over to where she felt the moist air moving over her throat. Without so much as trying to stop herself, she stripped off her clothes. Divesting herself of her underwear took the longest because nudity, especially nudity *he* demanded, made her feel incredibly exposed, but she had no choice or control over what her hands were doing. Finally, she stood with her shirt, shorts, bra, and panties pooled around her feet with her arms and legs spread and her head uplifted.

"What do you want?" she insisted. "Damn it, why are you doing this?"

"*You know.*"

Two words, two powerful words and her clitoris buzzed. "Because this is how you get your jollies."

"*No, not that.*"

"What then?"

His hands caressed her breasts.

"*Do you remember what happened between us?*" he asked.

"How can I possibly forget?"

His hands massaged her belly.

"I don't—damn it, I don't want you doing that."

"*Don't lie to me.*"

His hands explored her inner thighs.

"Laird, please!"

"*Soon you will be satisfied.*"

"You..." The last remnants of rational thought slipped away. Mindless, she arched her back and spread her legs, desperate to give him full access to the part of her that belonged to him anyway. With rough and confident fingers, he deftly separated her heated folds and probed deep inside her.

"Oh God, thank you."

"*Mine to do what I must with.*"

He was wrong. Her shuddering climax was her own.

But he'd made it possible.

Compelled it.

Thunder's lips curled into a smile. He pushed aside the small length of leather that was his only clothing and touched his swollen cock. In his mind, he saw the woman standing naked with her hands between her legs. Her head had fallen back, and her breath came in gasps. He smelled her body's juices and felt her uncontrolled spasms. Although he couldn't hear what she was saying, he read her lips. She was begging him, first to leave her alone, then to bring her to climax. He obeyed her command because that had been his intention from the beginning. She shuddered, jerked. Her mouth fell open and her limbs trembled. She cried.

Good. She would not forget his domination of her. Was that all he wanted from her? Wasn't there something more, something that had to do with his mouth gentle on her neck and wanting to feel her lips on his?

Posed to masturbate, he was distracted by an unfamiliar sound. Crouching, he cocked his head so he could better listen. Unfortunately, the swamp's song prevented him from distinguishing what didn't fit from the rest. Just the same, he drew his knife out of its leather sheath. According to the Seminole scouts he'd talked to earlier, a troop of perhaps a dozen soldiers had been camped near a large cypress swamp. As long as the enemy remained there, they represented no threat, but he had no doubt that they'd soon be on the move again. He had to shadow them and, if necessary, warn his people if the enemy got too close.

His cock was no longer as swollen as it had been a minute ago, but he still couldn't concentrate as fully as he should. He shook his head and sucked in hot, humid air that smelled of swamp gases and lush vegetation. Dimly he remembered other smells from the life he'd lived before joining his people, but those memories were fading. It was as it should be. He needed to become a Seminole warrior, nothing else.

Without warning, something slammed into his side. The force threw him forward and onto his knees, distracting him from a sharp rifle retort. Before he'd regained his breath, he fought his way back onto his feet. Strength was draining from him. His side screamed in pain. When he touched it, his hand became coated in blood.

Voices. Yelling. Too close.

Growling in shock and anger, Thunder stumbled toward several close-growing hardwood trees and hid behind the nearest one. Night was coming. Night might save him. His vision blurred, and when he tried to shake his head to clear it, agony dropped his legs out from under him. He slid onto his rump and hands, briefly losing his grip on his knife. Only half conscious now, he instinctively drew the knife to his chest. A minute, maybe two, then the worst of the pain would be over. He could think again.

Plan for survival.

Mala had taken the proverbial cold shower following her self-satisfaction and had managed to fall back into an uneasy sleep, but when consciousness returned, she wasn't surprised. After all, hadn't she learned, in spades, that getting free of Laird's particular brand of mind and body control wouldn't be easy?

Only—only what?

Sitting up, she turned on the lamp on her nightstand. The sudden light forced her to close her eyes until they adjusted. A quick inventory told her that, no, the man who now thought of himself as Thunder had no interest in getting her to play with herself again. Something else had made him reach out.

Something intertwined with pain.

Confused by the burning sensation in her side, she slipped out of bed and walked naked into the bathroom. A thorough examination reinforced what her searching fingers had already told her which was she had no injury there. And yet—damn, that hurt!

No, not her. Him.

Cold fear tightened her nipples and made swallowing difficult.

He was hurt.

Alone and vulnerable.

The long night had given way to day before Thunder felt fully conscious again. Hard as it was to manage his pain, he was thankful to it for clearing his head. From what he'd been able to determine, the bullet hadn't lodged itself in him. He'd felt no broken ribs, no sense that any vital organs had been pierced, but he'd lost a lot of blood and pressing leaves against his wound hadn't completely stopped the bleeding.

Like the hunted animal he'd been last night, he'd remained silent. He had foggy memories of hearing men and horses nearby, the hot taste of fear he'd never tell anyone about. When, finally, the enemy had ridden off, he'd given thanks to the spirits who'd protected him.

However, although he was fairly sure no one was waiting to ambush him, he had no delusions about the danger to his village. The soldiers had been on the move because they thought they knew where the Seminole fugitives were hiding. Because they foolishly insisted on traveling on horseback, they had to circumvent swampy areas and where vegetation grew too close together, but eventually they'd find the village.

He, Thunder, had to warn his people.

Weak, he had no choice but to frequently stop and rest. He berated himself for allowing himself to be distracted from his mission. At the same time, he refused to admit that weakness of the flesh had been solely responsible.

She—he couldn't remember her name—was evil. One of the enemy.

Gathering himself, he continued his lurching walk. He kept his hand against his side so his bandage would stay in place and had returned his knife to its sheath. His bow and quiver were still lashed to his back, but he didn't trust himself to be able to use the weapon. It would take a precious second to free the knife and have it at the ready, but he had no choice. Every step hurt. Every step increased his anger.

If he ever got his hands on *her* again, she'd wish she'd never been born. He'd fasten his hands around her neck and choke the life out of her, but not—but not until she'd felt the full fury of his rage. She thought him weak, did she? A man with a man's needs? A man enslaved by her sexual power?

Power was his!

It would be the last lesson she'd ever learn.

"Where are you?"

"I know you're here. Don't ask me how I do—or how I knew to come here. I did, and that's all that matters."

Frustrated by the sing-song inside her brain, Mala

clenched her fists. She felt fourteen kinds of a fool for having driven back into the damnable Everglades and repeating the too-familiar ritual of leaving her car and walking into the wilderness—in the middle of the night no less. She hadn't questioned why she'd taken off in a different direction this time with only the moon to guide her but could easily strangle whoever had decided she was up to crashing through endless plants. What was wrong with a path—even one created by wild animals? But no, Thunder was truly out in the middle of nowhere this time.

In the middle of nowhere, and hurt, she amended. She'd had enough presence of mind to pack a small first aid kit along with a bottle of water which, along with her practical tennis shoes, should have made her feel semi-in-control of the situation. Unfortunately, it didn't.

After all, there was no denying that this was the most insane thing she'd ever done.

Insane and frightening.

Vital.

As she slogged through yet another boggy area, she fought having to admit to what frightened her the most. Maybe believing Thunder had been wounded had only been a nightmare. If that was the case, she was out here for no reason—well, maybe the reason was she needed an excuse to find him so he could fuck her again.

Swell! When you get the hots for a man, you really go off the deep end.

Oh, hell! Was that it? She'd become his sex toy? *No.*

"Damn you, Laird, or Thunder, whatever you want to call yourself," she said because the depth of what she felt for him frightened her. "I don't need this. All right, I do not under any circumstances need this!"

"Yes, you do."

She'd lifted her left leg in preparation for stepping over a rotting log when something shoved her from behind. Throwing out her arms, she kept from falling by bracing herself against the log. She spun around, desperate to defend herself against her attacker.

Thunder! He launched himself at her like a panther leaps for its prey. His greater weight knocked her off balance. Together, they slid off the log. She landed on her back, pinned between the log and ground with an all but naked man now crouched over her.

"Laird!" she screamed although instinct told her the name meant nothing to him. "Laird, it's me!"

He growled deep in his throat. His menacing stance chilled her—but not enough that she didn't see his blood-soaked side. "I felt you," she said, fighting to keep her voice calm. "In my dreams and—you know."

His blazing eyes told her he cared about nothing except survival. At least he wasn't trying to kill her. This man had fucked her senseless, maybe even made love to her. That had to count for something, didn't it?

"What happened?" She indicated his side. "Who hurt you?"

From the way he was acting, she couldn't tell if he understood a word she'd said.

"That's what I felt, isn't it?" His reaction or lack of one didn't matter. She'd keep on talking because maybe something would get through to him. "I knew you'd been wounded. Maybe even without being aware of it, you sent me a message."

His next growl was lower, deeper.

"You haven't forgotten me. I'll never believe that." *Please, let that be true!* "And you won't hurt me." *But maybe you're not the man I let crawl inside me. Maybe he died.*

He stepped closer so that only a few inches separated them. Because she hadn't dared try to stand, she was forced to stare up at him. She'd landed on something sharp, but whatever was digging into her shoulder blade only briefly distracted her.

"I shouldn't have let you leave," she whispered. "Somehow I should have found a way to keep you with me. If I had, this wouldn't have happened." She nodded at his side. "But Laird—Thunder—whatever has hold of you is so powerful."

Words she didn't comprehend spewed out of him.

"Are the Seminole all right? You've been so worried about—about your people. The soldiers—is that who did this to you?"

He cocked his head to one side as if trying to understand. It suddenly dawned on her that they could be in danger. What if whoever had wounded him was nearby? She barely gave her own safety a thought, but Thunder's life was in danger. She had to get him out of here and into a hospital.

Propelled by a sense of purpose, she turned onto her side in preparation for getting onto her hands and knees. He rammed his hand against her shoulder, knocking her back again. Fury and fear warred inside her. She struggled to manage both emotions.

"I'm no threat to you. Surely you understand that."

He'd again assumed his aggressive stance, but even as she fought to ignore that, she became aware of his vulnerability. It wasn't just that she sensed his blood loss caused weakness. With his legs widespread, she had an almost unlimited view of his cock behind the loose, short loincloth. His cock wasn't swollen and hard, but neither was it limp.

"You've fucked me every way a woman can be fucked," she admitted. "Well, almost. Even when we weren't together, I felt you inside me. I was helpless to do anything about it, even more helpless than I am now. Everything you wanted me to do, I did. Now—now I want one thing from you."

He appeared to be listening. How much he comprehended, she couldn't say.

"Let me take care of you. Get you out of here."

His eyes darkened. His hand inched closer to his knife. Her mouth went dry. Unable to think of anything to say, she risked taking her gaze off him. The Everglades intruded from all sides, and the air was alive with the sound of countless unseen creatures. Humidity pressed down on her. For the life of her, she didn't know how she'd gotten here. Nothing mattered more than getting the hell out—with him.

Sucking in a deep breath, she reached up. Her hand closed around his cock. Calling herself insane, she nevertheless began stroking him. He started to draw back, then stopped. His cock swelled.

"You do remember," she whispered. Moving her fingers closer to his balls, she increased her hold on him. Her clitoris buzzed, but she clamped her legs together, determined to ignore her response. Then she noticed he was staring at what she'd done, and immediately spread herself wide.

"You want me," she said in a sing-song tone. "And I want you. Do it. Now."

Hoping to give weight to her words, she flexed her knees, looking for all the world as if she was preparing for a gynecological exam. "When you're done—when we've finished, I'll get you to a doctor."

She fully expected him to reach for her, but he didn't move.

"Why do you think I came all this way? Because I haven't had enough of you." *I'll never have enough of you.*

He continued to look down at her. Other than his engorged

penis, he seemed unaware of what she was doing to him.

"Thunder, please." Determined to get through to him, she reached for his necklace. Before she could touch it, however, he yanked his knife free of its sheath and dropped to the ground with his knees pressed against her lower legs. The movement tore his cock from her grasp. The knife was so close she couldn't see it clearly, knew only that he'd aimed it at her throat.

"No!"

Propelled by her scream, she threw out her hand, hoping to deflect the deadly blade. At the same time, she wrenched herself to the side. The knife was only inches from her throat, coming closer.

"No!"

Acting instinctively, she rammed her fist into his wounded side. He grunted and knocked her hand away. He'd become a blur—a blur now intent on slicing her throat open.

"Thunder, no!" she screamed. She pulled her leg tight up against her and let it fly. Her heel ground into his side.

He growled, then slumped to the ground.

Chapter Thirteen

When the cloud that had enveloped Thunder lifted, he noticed the woman before the pain in his side made its impact. There was something vaguely familiar about her, but she wasn't dressed like the women from his village and didn't smell like them. She was speaking to him, and he struggled to make sense of her strange words.

Instead of feeling like a trapped and helpless animal, he found himself being drawn to her. She held his knife and was far enough away that he couldn't reach it without getting to his feet—something he wasn't sure he was strong enough to accomplish. If only the side of his head where she'd hit him would stop throbbing.

"Sorry," she said. Then she repeated the word.

"So-rry?"

Her face lit up, and for a moment he thought she was going to embrace him. She didn't which left him wondering what his reaction would have been.

"That I hurt you," she said.

He blinked and started to shake his head but stopped when his headache worsened.

"You understand me?" she asked.

"Y-es."

"Thank goodness! How-how did that happen to you?" She pointed at his side.

He touched himself there, wincing as sweat from his hand burned the wound. "I do not know," he admitted.

"You don't remember?"

Everything was confusing. One thing he was positive about: he'd never admitted weaknesses to anyone. He wasn't going to start now, particularly not with this intriguing and disturbing woman.

"I'm not surprised." She spoke in a soothing voice, but there was nothing soothing about her impact on him. In truth, her every word touched a nerve ending. "You've been through so much."

He struggled to sit up. The effort stole his breath and left him panting in pain, but he completed the formidable task without accepting her outstretched hand. Now he was sitting with his weight mostly on his uninjured side. She scooted closer.

"Do you remember how we met?" she asked. Her left hand was only inches from his knees. The right held his knife and remained out of reach. "What's happened between us?"

A vague image of having seen her naked nagged at him. Even stronger was the sense that he'd had need of her and had capitalized on her lustfulness in order to achieve his goals. He wished he could remember how he'd accomplished that.

"Why are you here?" he asked. He hoped the question didn't reveal too much about his uncertain state of mind.

"Why? Because..." She raked her hand through her hair, then let it drop to her side. "Because you made me."

Another flash of memory struck, this one stronger and more vivid. He'd had sex with her. He was certain of that. She'd both resented the mating and had been hungry for it.

"Were you here when I was wounded?"

"No. If I had been, maybe it wouldn't have happened. I, ah, I know you by two names, Laird and Thunder. What do you want me to call you?"

Both names reminded him of well-loved songs. The first brought him closer to understanding who he'd always been while the other spoke of challenge, danger, and discovery. "You decide," he told her.

She frowned. "I never—Laird!" she said too emphatically. "That's who you are."

Once, maybe, but no longer. Unwilling to share his insight with her, he turned his thoughts inward. As long as he didn't move, he felt relatively clearheaded, but he doubted that would continue if he tried to stand. At the same time, he sensed that to stay here was dangerous. He rocked forward, his weight on his knees in preparation for getting to his feet. She must have guessed what he had in mind because she jumped up and positioned herself so he could cling to her if necessary.

He resented her confidence in her body and strength, but decided not to test the difference between them. Returning to a reclining position, he waited for her to kneel again. She did so, glaring at him.

The sense that he'd managed her earlier in ways that kept her off balance, aroused and angry at the same time, grew. Although he couldn't say where the conviction came from, he knew he'd always had a certain power over women and had used it to his advantage. Something was different about his connection to this one, but he didn't take the time to examine that.

"Who is Laird?" he demanded. "Tell me about him."

"You—you're him."

"I need to know who you believe he is."

Fury flashed in her eyes. She looked a breath away from striking him. Because he was in no condition to subdue her, he held out his hand, indicating he wanted her to place hers in it. For the first time, he noticed he was wearing a ring. He stared at it.

"It's mine," she said softly. "At least it was before I gave it to you. This—" She spun her bracelet around on her wrist so he could see all of it, "—was inspired by your necklace. You came to my place. I showed you the jewelry I make and gave you that ring. I-I called you Laird. You responded."

Just like he was responding now. Not caring that the loose flap of leather he wore didn't hide his growing erection, he reached out and boldly caught her right nipple between thumb and forefinger. Instead of pulling away, she leaned into him. A little of the fire in her eyes died to be replaced by a sheen of moisture.

"When I do this, what do you feel?" he asked.

"Don't make me say it."

Ignoring her plea, he rubbed until the nipple grew hard. It didn't take long.

"It isn't fair." Her voice sounded muffled. "You shouldn't—damn it!"

The throbbing in his side faded. Strength was returning to him, but whether it was enough to allow him to fuck her, he couldn't say. He tried to tell himself that getting at the truth of what today was about was more important, but until certain needs had been satisfied, until he'd stripped away her defenses and left her vulnerable, honest, and open—until he no longer felt alone—everything else would have to wait.

"What shouldn't I do?" he asked. If she'd wanted, she could have easily pulled free. Instead, she continued to lean into him with her neck arched as if she couldn't get enough oxygen into her lungs.

"That." She closed her fingers around his wrist.

"You do not like it."

"You know I do."

Yes, he did, just as he had no doubt of what she wanted from him. What he needed from her.

"I want you naked," he said. Although his cock throbbed, he released her and half turned his back on her, forcing her to let go of his wrist.

"Just—just like that?"

"Yes."

"Damn you, Laird. Sometimes I think this is the only thing we have going. It's a hell of a basis for a relationship. I want, damn it, I'd give anything for a little moonlight and roses from you. But do you even have a clue what I'm talking about?"

Even as she cursed him, she began lifting her shirt over her head. Her breasts popped free. They were generous but not so large that they hung down. He dug deep into his mind, asking if he'd seen them before, but he couldn't be sure—maybe because he had trouble thinking beyond his cock's urgent demand.

"I'm so confused when you do this to me," she said. She started to fold her arms across her breasts, then stopped.

"Then why do you?"

"What choice do I have?" She laughed bitterly. "And don't tell me you don't know what I'm talking about. I know you do."

He didn't respond, only stared at her. His hands rested on his knees. Between them, his swollen cock waited.

Mala swallowed and tried to take her eyes off the too-familiar shaft. This was hardly the first time he'd played his damnable game with her—if that's what it was. And it certainly wasn't the first time she'd lost contact with her body. It existed beyond her control, his plaything.

And yet if fucking him meant getting him out of here and to a hospital and safety, it was worth it. Beneath that savage exterior was a man who understood what her craft meant to her, who laughed and loved sea breezes. Clinging to that excuse for what she was about to do, she put down the knife and scooted closer. She thought his hands twitched, but maybe she only imagined that his need equaled hers. He'd been silent for what seemed like a long, long time, and yet, much as she loved the sound of his voice, it was better this way.

Or it would have been if ropes of sexual desire hadn't wrapped around her.

When her knees brushed his, she ran her hands up his thighs. Doing that threw her slightly off balance and forced her to lean forward. Now her breasts dangled, and her nipples felt like hot rocks. Hungry in a way no food could ever satisfy, she cupped her hands under her breasts and lifted them toward him. Already, sweat slickened her palms. Maybe he smiled but maybe she only imagined his superior grin. He didn't take her offering.

"What do I have to do?" she demanded. Her lips felt both numb and over-sensitized. "Don't you want me?"

He remained silent and still. Gathering courage and clamping down on her anger at the same time, she looked him in the eye. His nostrils flared and his hands had become fists. His penis strained against the soft loincloth. But despite those cues, his eyes revealed confusion and doubt.

Were the Seminole trying to take control of him?

Fearful of what that meant to their safety, she slid even closer, forcing him to widen his stance so she fit between his legs. She wanted to throw her weight at him and force him back onto the ground, for once have the upper hand in this damnable battle of theirs, but didn't dare risk injuring him further. Instead, she curled down upon herself with her butt sticking out until her mouth reached his cock. She considered taking him into her and giving him head he'd never recover from, but this moment was about more than satisfying him—much more.

Her lips were swollen, much like his penis. Although she felt the strain along the back of her neck, she rested her hands on his thighs and stretched out to kiss the head she knew intimately. He shuddered and sucked in hot air but that, she told herself, was involuntary and not an effort to escape her. She couldn't see him clearly, but that didn't matter. She didn't need sight.

"I want this to be good," she whispered. "Not just some roll in the hay, but great sex. Beyond sex and fucking. Lovemaking."

Again and again, slow and deliberate, she feathered his throbbing cock with light kisses. In the past—such as it was—she'd handled him roughly, He was, after all, a rough and rugged man. But for reasons she didn't dare explore, she no longer thought of him that way. Fucking was for strangers who wanted nothing more than the proverbial roll in the hay.

Making love was different. Deeper.

His cock dripped. She lapped at the moisture and drew it into her mouth, tasted it and him. She no longer felt the strain in her neck. How could she with her body whirring and hot? Wet heat pooled around the lips of her cunt, and everything down there felt swollen. She pressed her legs together, not to try to kill the fire but, damn it, she still wore clothes.

Thinking maybe she could distract herself from the building pressure, she renewed her efforts. After repositioning herself, she turned her attention to his scrotum. She closed her lips over her teeth and nipped at whatever loose flesh she could reach. He again sucked in a breath and shoved his fingers through her hair. She felt a tug, but if he was trying to get her to stop, he'd have to do better than that.

Her rump still stuck up in the air. Despite the hated fabric, she felt—or imagined she did—a hot breeze dance along her butt cheeks. So much for dismissing her own needs!

Resigned to dealing with sexual frustration, she moistened her tongue before running it over and around his balls. They contracted up into him, prompting her to chuckle. His grip on her hair tightened. She welcomed the pain.

Unexpectedly, her shoulder muscles protested the awkward position she'd put them in, and she fell forward. If his thighs hadn't been there, she would have landed on her nose on the ground. As it was, she could barely breathe with said nose smashed against his solid muscle.

Instead of helping her straighten, he slid his hands inside the back of her waistband and clamped his fingers around her rump. The absurdity of what they were doing made her laugh. At least she did until her inability to draw a full breath forced her to turn her head to the side. The top of her head pressed against his belly, and his cock grazed her cheek.

She stuck out her tongue and licked. He "rewarded" her by pressing his fingertips into her rump and dimpling it. Her pussy grew hotter, wetter, even more swollen. She spread her legs as far apart as possible and entertained the fantasy of anal sex.

Instead of taking advantage of her unspoken invitation, he pulled his hands out from inside her shorts. Feeling abandoned, starving for more, she tried to sit up. Before she could pull it off, he grabbed her shoulders and forced her face back down to his crotch.

So much for lovemaking!

A heartbeat later, she changed her mind. She offered no resistance when he unbuttoned her shorts and slipped them down over her butt. Now her cheeks were truly waving in the wind. He reached over and around and down her ass and touched—just barely touched—her swollen labial lips. Her passage overflowed, and moisture dribbled from her. Already a climax thrummed, demanded, promised.

When he left off stimulating her there and ran his fingers over her anus, she did the only thing she was capable of. Eyes squeezed shut against the real world, she opened her mouth around his cock and drew him as far as possible inside her.

She couldn't think clearly, wasn't certain she was pleasuring him in the way he deserved. His forefinger pressed against her anus, wiggled and probed. Both fighting and encouraging her own climax, she sucked. He was big, so big! How could she—how could she not do all she could to provide his cock with a home?

What—what had she promised? Lovemaking, more than just sex.

But this—God, it felt good!

The world behind her eyelids became midnight. Even as one hand continued to test the entrance to her butt hole, Laird used his other hand to slide two fingers past her labial lips and into her throbbing opening. She felt herself empty out and engorge at the same time, relaxed her pussy and welcomed him in, drenched him with her fluids. And then, and then—yes!—a fingertip kissed her clit. A deep shudder rammed through her. Nearly there. Almost—

Barely conscious, she pressed her own fingers against Laird's groin, then switched to a rubbing motion. His cock jerked inside her mouth. She sucked until she felt his wet, sticky head against the back of her throat.

Together. We'll get off together.

Oh my—his fingers in me. Finding the switch. Playing with it. Turning it on. My mouth housing his cock. Together! Damn, damn, together!

No!

Yanked back from the brink, Mala was slow to comprehend that Laird had shoved her away. His cock slipped noisily out of her.

Panting, she braced her hands on his thighs but couldn't yet summon the strength and presence of mind to sit up. Her shorts, still tangled around her knees, felt like bonds.

A man spoke. In Seminole.

Laird answered.

Shaking and breathless, she glanced over her shoulder.

The old man from her dream—the one Laird called Osceola—stood looking down at them. He'd folded his hands over his slightly sunken chest. His eyes blazed. He spoke softly, all but ignoring her. Laird listened intently and occasionally nodded. She'd never wanted anything as much as she wanted to have him tell her everything was all right, but it wasn't going to happen.

"Laird," she managed around the constriction in her throat. "What does he want?"

Giving no indication that he'd heard, Laird stood. He clamped his hand over his side, letting her know what that had cost him. She grabbed his ankle, then lifted herself enough to press her cheek against his hard leg.

"Laird, don't forget me. Please."

With no sign that he was the least bit embarrassed about how Osceola had found them, Laird repositioned his loincloth so it covered him before walking over to Osceola and lowering his head. The chief pressed his palm against Laird's forehead, then wrapped his loose-skinned arms around Laird's shoulders and pulled him against him.

Mala sobbed low in her throat. Her body still screamed from unrelieved sexual tension. It was all she could do to not to jam her fingers up inside her cunt and satisfy herself. But if she did, the risk of losing Laird forever would become even greater.

Only maybe Laird Jaeger was dead.

Replaced by Thunder.

Chapter Fourteen

"The men who shot you are scouts. They did not stay to hunt you down because they want to return to the others and guide them to the village."

With awful clarity, Mala clung to what the sick-looking Seminole chief was telling Laird—Thunder. Why she could suddenly understand him didn't matter.

"How many are there of our enemy?" Thunder asked. He stood taller than he had a moment ago and seemed to have forgotten his wound.

"Hundreds. Maybe a thousand."

Mala shuddered. She believed, fully, what Thunder had told her about the small village with no more than twenty warriors. What would happen to those women, children, and the elderly if those twenty warriors were killed or captured?

"A thousand." Thunder's voice carried no hint of fear. "They will travel together, right?"

Osceola nodded. "It is their way. Them and their horses."

Mala pulled up her shorts and fastened them. She glanced around for her shirt. Not spotting it, she promptly forgot about it. What did naked breasts matter when a determined and well-armed army was coming for the Indian fugitives?

Thunder nodded, indicating he heard the chief's every

word. "That many men and animals cannot move silently. Before they reach us, we will know. And if I stay near them as they travel, spy—"

"Thunder!" she interrupted. She hurried over to him but didn't try to touch him. "They already shot you once."

He threw a glance her way before returning his attention to Osceola. "It will not happen again."

She might have called him boastful if it hadn't been for the dark, powerful determination in his eyes. Although she should care about nothing except making sure he stayed alive, she couldn't keep her eyes off Osceola. He was taller than she'd expected. The paintings she'd seen of him hadn't done him justice. His mouth was soft, almost feminine, but his square, strong jaw downplayed that as did his piercing black eyes. His nose was long and straight, his large ears barely covered by long, thick gray hair. Unlike the nearly naked Thunder, he was dressed in a long sleeved shirt, a loose, knee-length skirt and leather leggings. He wore a necklace made from three large turtle shells and carried a rifle. Right now he was using the rifle to lean against. His face looked flushed and his eyes were red-rimmed, probably from a fever. No wonder he was asking Thunder to take charge.

Nevertheless, she couldn't remain silent. "He's wounded," she told the chief. "I know you're sick, but he's no better."

Osceola gave her naked breasts the briefest glance before locking his gaze on her. "Thunder's wound is nothing. He will ignore it."

"How do you—"

"Mala, don't!"

Stung by her lover's warning, she clamped her hand over her mouth. He looked so damn magnificent! Proud, determined, strong despite the blood loss.

"I must do this," he went on almost softly. "Surely you understand."

No, I don't! I never will! Do you think—I'm afraid for you. Don't you understand that?

"I can no longer lead," Osceola said. "Thunder's time has come."

"We—my people and I—are not animals waiting to be hunted down," Thunder continued. "The Everglades will shelter us. We will survive."

What about me?

"His spirit is strong," Osceola went on. "Eagle and panther give him their courage."

"I embrace their courage." Thunder nodded at Osceola. "I will make it mine."

He already had. That's what she'd fallen in love with. Not just wanted to screw, fallen in love with.

Mala's legs trembled so she could barely force herself to walk toward Thunder. She didn't remember him being this tall or so heavily muscled. Maybe the only thing she truly recognized was what dangled between his legs. Her body continued to scream a denial of what she was about to do, but she listened to her heart.

"Yes," she whispered. "You will." Reaching up, she flattened her hands against his chest. Beneath flesh and bone, his heart beat. Despite the awful cost, she met his gaze. "You're the Seminoles' hope, their only chance for a future."

He didn't say anything, but she didn't expect him to, didn't think she could survive hearing his voice on top of everything else. She slid her hands up and over his breasts and wrapped them around his neck. He bent toward her and hugged her to him.

The tears she'd been afraid she couldn't hold back died. She'd never been prouder of anyone than she was of him at this moment. An image swam into her mind, allowing her to see the collection of simple grass huts. Babies and toddlers lay in their parents' arms or played under the shade the roofs afforded while women and the elderly occupied themselves with food preparation or making clothes. Boys who'd barely reached adolescence had stationed themselves at the edge of the clearing and served as guards. The village's men were huddled together in a tight circle, talking intently. They were all armed.

"You see them," Thunder whispered. It wasn't a question.

"Y-es."

"And you understand?"

A baby started to cry. A young woman put down the shoes she'd been fashioning from leather and grasses, picked up the infant and placed her breast in its mouth.

"Yes," she said. "I understand."

Her throat clogged. She swallowed and again looked up at Thunder. He lowered his head toward her, inviting.

Crying silently, she pressed her mouth against his. Her lips were slightly parted, as were his, but she didn't try to thrust her tongue into him. Their first and last true kiss shouldn't be just about sex. Instead, she'd leave him with the message of her love for him.

Their embrace deepened. She felt him from breasts to legs, melted into him, and made him part of her. Then, made strong by him, she pushed back. Tears spilled over and ran down her cheeks, but she ignored them.

"Go," she whispered. "They need you more than I do."

He nodded. She couldn't read his expression. Insane as it was, she still wanted him to tell her he'd chosen her over responsibility and danger, but he didn't. Instead, he stepped away from her and loosened the drawstring on his necklace. Reaching into it, he pulled out a small, white feather which he handed to her. Her fingers didn't shake as she took it and pressed it into the hollow between her breasts.

I love you.

Naked from the waist up, Mala stepped out of the Everglades. The wind had picked up and the sky had taken on a purple hue. The air felt charged. Traffic whizzed past, people staring at her, the smell and sound sickening her. She didn't look up but concentrated on putting one leaden foot after another as she trudged toward her car. It was unlocked, the key in the ignition. She supposed she should have been grateful that no one had stolen it, but it didn't matter. Neither did she care that her breasts were exposed.

When she opened the door, heated air rushed from it. She vaguely remembered having water with her when she went into the wilderness but had no idea what had happened to it. Her mouth was dry, and her stomach rumbled. After sliding behind the wheel, she started the car, turned on the air conditioning and looked in the rear view mirror in preparation for pulling onto the highway.

Something dark and sleek was coming her way—a motorcycle! Uttering a sharp cry, she whirled around. A moving van rumbled past in the right hand lane. An older car with the back seat piled high with belongings and a tired looking female driver tailed behind the van. The rest of the vehicles were in the left lane. There was no motorcycle.

Mala's head dropped forward, and she hit her forehead on the steering wheel. Tears sprang to her eyes, but she fought them. If she didn't, she might never stop crying.

Straightening, she reached for the gear shift. As she did, her gaze fell on her wrist and the new bracelet—the bracelet she'd created using Thunder's necklace as inspiration. Instead of shifting into Drive, she removed the bracelet and let it dangle from her fingers. Then she dug into the pocket of her shorts and pulled out the white feather he'd given her. She put the two items together, not surprised to see the bracelet wrap partly around the feather.

Sighing, she rolled down the windows and turned off the engine. Next—not allowing herself to think about what she was doing—she pushed the driver's seat back as far as it would go, unfastened her shorts and slipped her hand between her legs. She closed her eyes and let the back of her head flop against the head rest.

Creating jewelry had been her life—the only thing she'd ever really cared about.

But that had been before a man—Thunder—had come into that pitiful excuse for a life.

She was still hot from those moments spent in his arms. Still felt his fingers inside her throbbing crotch, teasing her nether lips, igniting her clit.

Claiming her. Owning her.

Showing her what it is to be a woman.

A woman who didn't belong in her man's world—who might not survive it.

What was better, a lifetime of lonely self-satisfaction or hiding from the enemy and maybe seeing her lover die?

Rain sluiced down the trees and soaked the ground. Some of the droplets struck Mala, but getting wet was the last thing on her mind. Her legs ached because she'd run back to where she'd last seen Thunder. Despite her speed, however, neither man was here. Confused, she shoved the toes of her shoes into the carpet of vegetation at her feet. She'd been thirsty before she'd started her run. Now her mouth felt as if had been packed with cotton.

Inspiration struck, and she walked over to a tree, cupped a large leaf into a bowl shape and watched raindrops dribble into it. When it was full, she drank. Thinking to repeat the task, she pulled the leaf free and placed it under a rivulet sliding off another tree. Filling the leaf this time only took a few seconds, but it still left her with enough time to ask what she should do next. She'd trusted her instinct to guide her to the village, but what if Thunder didn't want her?

What if soldiers found her?

Half sick with fear, she held the leaf to her mouth. No way could she lie to the soldiers and tell them she was anything except a Seminole lover—their new chief's lover. They'd find that out and force her to—

Something slammed into her back, pitching her face first onto the ground. The wind was knocked out of her. She felt as if she was being pressed into the sodden ground. Before she could decide whether to give into fear, curse, or demand an explanation, she glimpsed long, hairy legs out of the corner of her eye.

"Thunder! It's me."

For maybe five seconds, he said or did nothing. She waited, hoping against hope that he'd roll her over and complete what they'd started before Osceola interrupted. Instead, he held out his hand, indicating he'd help her to her feet. She grasped his hand and stood. Looking down at herself, she wasn't surprised to find her wet top covered with leaves. Her breasts stood at attention.

"I-I came back."

He merely nodded and then released her. Taking a backward step, he regarded her. Remnants of civilization had clung to him the last time she'd seen him, but since then he'd become part and parcel of the wilderness. Someone had tied a bandage around his middle. He carried a spear and wore some kind of cloth cap with three large feathers sticking out of it. A crude outline of a panther had been painted on his chest. She'd never seen a man look this magnificent, this formidable.

"This is your world," she managed. "You'll never go back to what you were before, will you?"

He barely shook his head, but then he didn't have to.

"I, ah, I couldn't leave."

"I will not leave here with you. I cannot." He sounded proud, yet resigned, maybe even sad.

"I know. Laird—I don't know if the name means anything to you—but that's what your brother calls you. I left him a message in my car and others for my parents and best friend. I told your brother he can do what he wants with your business. You won't be back. I also told him not to worry because you were doing what was right for yourself. I wrote pretty much the same thing to Sandy and my parents."

Her throat caught at the thought of what no longer having her in their lives would mean to them. "I told my mother and father not to mourn me, that I have no doubts about what I'm doing. That I found the man I want to spend the rest of my life with, but we'd be living that life in a place they can never come to. I'll find ways to stay in touch with them, and if they ever need me, I'll be there."

There was so much more she could say about decisions made and freedom of will, but it didn't matter. Her attention caught on the ring she'd given him. "You're still wearing it."

"Yes."

"Why?"

"Because I like it."

"I'm, ah, I'm glad to hear that." *Stop it! This isn't the time for waffling!* "Thunder, fashioning jewelry is everything to me, at least it used to be. If I'm not creating something, I feel incomplete."

If only he'd give some indication he gave a damn about what she was saying. But maybe he was testing her, forcing everything to come out of her.

"I thought I knew the meaning of the word incomplete until I got into my car a few minutes ago," she continued. "But even when I couldn't give away my creations, it didn't hurt the way—the way it did when I realized I'd never see you again."

"So you returned."

"Yes."

He took a backward step. Terrified he'd leave her, she hurried on. "Not because I was determined to bring you back with me. I tried that. It didn't work."

He continued to stare at her in that intense but remote way of his.

"Thunder, the world that exists beyond here doesn't matter to you. I know it. And—it doesn't to me, either." She felt weak. Had she really come to this place in her life, this decision? Risking everything, she approached him and took his finger, the one with her ring on it. "My art is part of me. That will never change, but I don't have to live in a little house with a shop. I can create anywhere. What I can't do is live without you."

There. She'd said it. Stripped herself naked.

"You want me to say the same?" he asked. "I cannot."

"I know."

"I want to," he whispered. "But I cannot."

"Because it isn't just you anymore."

His dark eyes told her she was right.

"I understand that," she admitted. "Accept it. And—and if you'll have me, I'm ready to walk into that world with you."

For the first time since they'd met, he looked defenseless. "No doubts?" he asked.

"No doubts."

He pulled his finger free, then wrapped his arms around her. She burrowed into him, smelled his earthy smell and felt his awesome power. Even as she stood on tiptoe and lifted her head to kiss him, her nerve endings stirred. She felt his equal response. Soon, soon they'd make love.

Their kiss went on and on, tongues reaching out and probing, pelvises grinding together, breathing hard to control. And yet, no matter how eager she was to feel him deep inside her, she could wait.

Finally her calf muscles cramped, and she lowered herself. When she opened her eyes, she first hungrily took in his masculine features, but then her awareness of her surroundings returned, and she looked around.

People were walking toward them. A boy of about five or six was in the lead. A woman she took to be his mother was behind him, and she carried a baby on her hip. A moment later, those three were joined by others who seemed to glide out of the wilderness and take form. Most were burdened with belongings. They looked, not fearful, but proud and determined. One after another, they inclined their heads in Thunder's—their chief's—direction.

Wonder at having fully joined him in the Seminole world rendered her speechless. Only a short while ago she wouldn't have believed this was possible. There was no such thing as going back in time.

But that was before her life had been turned on end.

Before Thunder's priorities had become hers.

Thunder's arm was still around her when she reached out and the woman handed the baby to her.

"Does that mean," she whispered, "that they accept me?"

"You are my woman. They understand that." He bent to kiss the top of the baby's head.

The touching gesture brought tears to her eyes. She rested her head on his shoulder.

"I have so much to learn," she said as he held the baby away from her so the girl could study her. "So many things I want to know."

"It is a journey we will take together."

Pulling his words into her heart, she smiled. "That's why I came back. Because no matter what the future brings, I need to live it with you. I want to with all my heart."

"No more than I need and want you." He leaned close and pressed his lips against the side of her neck. "Forever."

About the Author

Night Hunter is Vonna Harper's third erotic romance with Samhain. Writing since dirt was new, she has no other marketable skills beyond lawn mowing, weeding, and minor computer repair. A dedicated country hick, she's married with two sons, four grandchildren, two dogs, assorted lizards, wild turkeys, and deer. (Don't ask.) Please visit her at www.vonnaharper.com.

To tame a wild thing, first you must gain her trust.

Predator
© 2011 Vonna Harper

Mia's retreat on Cougar Mountain was supposed to be a quiet time of communing with nature. Instead, she can't shake the sense she's being watched. The reason why appears before her, chilling her to the bone. His name is Stark. And he says he's been waiting for her.

She takes to her heels, but it does no good. Captured and bound, she is surprised to feel no fear. Instead, she is mesmerized as her soul drinks deeply of his dark, commanding sexuality.

Stark once fought the Cougar Spirits, but now he embraces their mission to protect the forest and its creatures. Mia is his destined mate, perfectly made to fight by his side. But first he must tame her, starting with a slow and relentless seduction of her body—while he reveals each painful bit of his past.

Mia finds herself sinking into his touches, seeing the world as he sees it. But as shots ring out in the forest, she sees something else. A vision that Stark may never understand...and could not only destroy the bare beginnings of their destined love, but their mission to save the wilderness.

Warning: Sharp teeth and powerful male muscles, a watching, waiting cougar, enough heat to catch the woods on fire.

Available now in ebook from Samhain Publishing.

Enjoy the following excerpt for Predator:

He approached, and yet he didn't. There was no other way of explaining what she was seeing. Yes, his legs moved, but not with a simple and practiced bending of the knees and flexing of muscles. Instead, he glided, slid, floated toward her. Maybe her reaction was connected to the mountain's name, but it seemed that his progress mirrored that of a big cat—effortless, powerful and supremely confident.

Something shifted inside her, a sloughing off of restraint and caution. Instead of being ruled by the instinct for survival, an equally primal response pushed its way to the surface. For the first time in her life, she wanted, simply wanted, a man. Wanted to grab and hold on, to crush her mouth against his, to pull his scent into her and run her lips over his belly. To scream as he mounted her.

Her cheeks and throat heated. Her senses sharpened and narrowed at the same time until little existed except the human life-form closing the distance between them. He became more than three-dimensional, an exquisite Greek god. She mentally stripped off his clothing. He smelled of the earth and sun and more: skin and clean hair. Lips buzzing and thighs trembling, she fought the instinct to wrap her arms and legs around him and invite his body into hers.

Not an animal! Damn it, not some bitch in heat!

Closer, his heat beginning to seep into her and now within easy reach. Bombarded by opposing emotions, she swung between surrendering to his male strength and running as she'd never run. "Stop. Not another step."

"Too late." Despite his words, he ceased his graceful-as-hell gliding and settled his arms at his sides. "It became too late the moment you decided to come here."

Oh, shit. "Who are you?"

Instead of answering, his remarkable eyes began a slow journey down her body. Unnerved by the intense scrutiny, she nevertheless took note of his eye color. From a distance, the black had predominated, but now she saw yellow flecks dancing in the darkness. She'd never seen eyes like that, certainly not on a human. For an instant, she thought she'd come up with the creature they reminded her of, but that slid away when his gaze settled on her crotch.

Her crotch, the center of her sexuality, was short-circuiting. She couldn't simply say she was turned on, because the sensations were more intense and nearly uncontrollable. Fighting not to squeeze her legs together, she wondered if he could sense her arousal.

Of course he did! That's why he was staring at that part of her anatomy. "Look, I don't appreciate this damn game you're playing. The rest of my group's close by. All I have to do is pick up my cell phone, and they'll be here."

"You're alone. Like me."

Oh, shit. "Fine. Whatever. But just because we are doesn't mean I'm yours for the—whatever you're thinking. I know how to defend myself."

She knew this land; at least, she comprehended the pulse of the wilderness. But she wasn't fool enough to trust everyone who shared it with her. If not for the primitive heat between them, she'd have already put distance between her and the stranger. Wouldn't she?

A nod of his head distracted her. He was so damn sexy, all male energy and promise, dangerous as hell. "Don't be afraid of me," he said. "I'm not going to hurt you."

"Of course you aren't. I won't let you."

"You're brave. That's good."

Throat dry, she wrenched her awareness off her pussy and

glanced behind her to make sure she had a path to freedom. "You're not making any kind of sense, and I've had enough of whatever the hell this is."

"It's destiny, what the spirits have ordained."

Cougar Spirits? Enough! God damn enough! Not so much as blinking, she slid her right hand into her rear pocket and extracted her knife. It opened with a soft click, the blade aimed at his throat. "I don't know or care what damn spirits you're talking about. This conversation has gone on more than long enough. You go your way, and I'll go mine."

"I can't let that happen."

The words hit her like drumbeats. There was more than a little wildness to him, as if he was driven by instinct instead of his mind. What if he had no control over his actions, was dangerous?

She took a backward step, and then another. Her gaze remained fixed on him. He didn't move, didn't breathe. And he didn't seem surprised by her actions. A few more steps brought her close to a thicket. To the right of it grew a number of widely spaced evergreens. As long as she watched her footing, she could easily navigate her way around the trees.

Could run.

Sucking in the oxygen she'd need for the task, she spun on her heels and leaped into the shadows. Her backpack dragged on her shoulders and back, and she unhooked the straps that fastened it to her chest and waist. If need be, she'd discard the pack and run full-out.

A sound, a growl, something coming from deep inside a man or animal's chest, sounded behind her. Her nerve endings told her he was coming after her. Not taking time for the scream that ached to erupt, she shrugged out of her pack and flung it aside. Her pistol was in it, but at least she had her knife.

Could she use it on Mountain Man?

Before she could reach top speed, he wrapped his arms around her waist and lifted her off the ground. She dangled for precious seconds before digging her nails into his forearms. "Stop it!" she screamed. "Damn you, don't!"

Not letting go, he lowered her to the ground and forced her onto her knees. When he hit the ground beside her, she renewed her efforts to tear out of his hold. Although she drew blood, his grip remained strong, making it hard to breathe.

He was trying to force her onto her belly! Terrified and furious, she wrenched to the side. Too late she realized she'd released her hold on his forearms.

"God damn you!"

He seemed to be everywhere, blanketing her, pushing her down. Her breath whistled, and her muscles screamed as she struggled, but she was no match for him. The ground pressed against her breasts.

"What the hell are you doing?" she demanded, although she already knew. He didn't answer.

Bending her knees, she tried to kick him, but he straddled her, his weight imprisoning her thighs. At the same time, he pushed down on her shoulder blades, making it impossible for her to do more than lift her head. Her left arm was caught under her, the right at her side. She managed to slide her right arm upward, but found nothing to grip.

"Let me go!"

"I can't."

Lying under him like some trapped wild animal was unacceptable, so she twisted and squirmed. Panic clawed, and sweat coated her skin. So heavy, so damn solid! It would take little for him to crush the life out of her. She was still struggling, albeit with lessened strength, when he stopped pressing on her back. She managed to turn her head a little more, then wished she hadn't, because he was removing his own backpack and reaching into it.

"This is insane. I'll charge you with—you know I will."

When he held up a length of rope, she screamed. And screamed again, her voice spiraling into the trees.

No! Not rope being tied around her *free* wrist! But although she fought the restraint with everything in her, he easily tied it in place. Then, using the loose end to hold her arm up behind her, he pulled her trapped arm out from under her. She fought the inevitable, fought and swore and screamed again, but he easily lashed her wrists together.

Not content with rendering her arms useless, he slid off her and grabbed the ankle next to him. Despite her resistance, he bent her knee up so her heel rested on her buttocks and hogtied her ankle to her wrists. It mattered little that he'd left enough slack that she wasn't in danger of losing circulation. What could she do with only one free leg?

Still on his knees, he scooted away. Rolling onto her side as best she could, she locked her gaze on him. Much as she needed to scream, she feared that would enrage him. He stared back at her, his expression unreadable. Her heart beat like thunder, and yet an emotion she refused to acknowledge calmed and quieted what could have become panic. Every inch of her was alert and alive and focused on her beautiful captor.

"What do you want?" she asked when his silence became more than she could stand. "Damn it, what is this about?"

"It's about following our destiny."

One act of kindness cements a destiny she couldn't fathom.

Wolf
© *2010 Cara Carnes*
An *Enchanted* story.

As a child, the Lost Woods were Hannah's passion. A place where she dreamed of mysterious creatures, including one she saved—a man who magically changed into a wolf. Now, twelve years later, the woods are her refuge from a horde of marauders who killed her mother.

This time, it is the wolf who saves her. And he is no dream.

Stephan can't help but remember the time Hannah encouraged him to free his injured leg and continue the soul journey required of his kind. The child unwittingly bound herself to him, and now the woman tempts him like no other. Yet if she learns his secret, her fragile trust could be broken for all time.

Hannah doesn't see how she can possibly fit into Stephan's world—especially when their overwhelming passion reveals the one reason she should not trust him. Stephan has fought more than his share of battles, but the one for Hannah's heart is the one that could break his own...

Warning: Kickass, shape-shifting alphas will leave you breathlessly begging for Lost Woods. Be careful...they may know what you think!

Available now in ebook and print from Samhain Publishing.

Enjoy the following excerpt for Wolf:

Stephan.

My pulse quickened and I fiddled with the hem of my borrowed dress. I gawked at his powerful body as he greeted Nalla. His eyes danced with adoration when around her, and I wished I could see the same glimmer in his eyes when he thought of me.

The same type of clinging leather pants molded against his powerful thighs. Muscle rippled across his stomach, partially visible through the open wood-colored vest. His chest was unmarred by hair. My fingers longed to trace the contours of his smooth skin.

Heat spread through me to center at my nether regions. I squeezed my thighs together and looked down because I was afraid my cheeks were stained with shame. My attraction to him had grown, and my body refused to behave.

His long legs brought him to me faster than I was prepared for. I stood, my legs wobbling as my breathing accelerated. His hands grasped my arms, steadying me with a strength that made me shiver. Not even the mightiest of my village's fighters were so honed and muscular. I'd seen enough of his people to know none of the men in his pride were like the men I was accustomed to.

"Thanks."

Thanks. Not only was it a naïve and foolish thing to say, but it came out with a meekness that made my mind scream at my blathering tongue. I'd thought of clever retorts and envisioned conversations with him about many things for the past few nights. I'd even fantasized about him.

And all I had to say when he stood before me was "thanks". A flicker of darkness appeared and disappeared in his golden eyes.

Nalla shuffled a chair. The dragging sound across the bare floor of the eating area pulled me from my lustful thoughts. I focused my attention to where his fingers touched my skin. Tingles danced there and spread through me like molten fire. Heat rushed to my core. My pussy moistened. My nipples hardened.

I fought the urge to tug on my dress or look down to see if it was apparent. I refused to sever my contact with him.

"She's been asking about you." Nalla's voice quashed the connection I'd felt. I stepped back enough to allow my heartbeat to slow, but his assessing gaze remained on me, and I was lost in the tumbling waves of desire his presence had incited.

"Really?" His voice, filled with curiosity, made me smile. "I've been catching up on pride issues. Some of it is quite tedious. I'm sure your company would have broken up the monotony."

"She has a restless spirit, much like you." Nalla chuckled. "Were she one of us, she'd be prowling in animal form."

Stephan grinned. I couldn't understand their amusement, but I knew she had no ill regard for me. She sat at the table and regarded us.

"Is her leg healing well?" he asked.

I hadn't realized how injured my leg was until Nalla had begun treating it. "Those poultices of hers don't burn anymore. Surely that's a good sign."

Nalla laughed. The rich tones of her wise voice soothed me. I hadn't realized I missed my gran until that moment. They were too alike for me not to be drawn to her.

"She's been asking about your talisman and wanted to walk the village. Perhaps you can appease her."

"Sure." His voice was low. "I'll gladly tell her why she has our talisman and what it represents."

"Your father wouldn't approve."

"Then it's a good thing I stopped heeding his advice long ago. If anyone has need of me, send Fallon for me."

Fallon. "He's your brother, right?"

"I see you've been learning of my family. I trust Nalla's delighted in telling you many stories of my foolish youth."

I wished that was the case. The woman had offered nothing.

"I will, now that I see you approve."

Stephan chuckled and touched my arm. The contact made my skin tingle. "Let us go before she starts now."

His arm rested on my back just above my waist. Cool air whipped through my hair when we exited the home I'd been locked away in. Unable to contain my glee, I paused and took a deep breath.

"I should've come sooner, but Nalla kept telling me you needed to heal."

"She's very protective."

"It's in her blood. Women in my clan have been healers for many generations." His hand fell away from me when we began to walk through his village.

Everyone halted their activities as we passed. I found their scrutiny disconcerting. The first few moved to their knees as if about to undertake a chore I didn't understand. All the homes we passed resembled one another. Most displayed a talisman on the entry.

I tried to study them without being obvious, but decided it best not to when Stephan drew me closer to him.

"Your people don't like me."

"They're unaccustomed to strangers. There's a difference." The sincerity calmed my nervousness even though I doubted it was the truth for everyone.

"I've heard some of them yelling at Nalla." I winced when his jaw twitched. "She tries to hide it, but I hear them. They want me gone."

"She should have told me this. I would've dealt with their meddling myself."

I shook my head. "They have a right to be upset. I'm doing nothing to earn my keep and am not of your pride."

We continued our path toward the woods and my pulse quickened when I realized he didn't intend to remain within the village. A few awkward smiles greeted me once we neared a group of homes with the same talisman that I wore around my neck.

"This is your family's area?"

He nodded. "On my father's side."

"Why isn't Nalla here? She displays this talisman, yet is on the other side of the village."

"She's on my mother's side, but may display whichever talisman she feels within her soul since she's a healer. She's chosen this one since it's stronger than her other option."

"Do all your kind get that option?"

"Only the healers or those within the royal line." His hand returned to my back and drew me toward him until my thigh brushed his as we walked. "You gather information well." My mind swelled with his admiration.

He paused and turned me to face him. His attention moved to the village, now a good distance from our secluded cove. I was fascinated by the large tree misshapen by time. Its trunk was hollowed near the base. A small sitting stool rested within the area.

"This is my retreat."

"It's beautiful."

His fingers grazed my cheek. My heart flailed in my chest. He'd brought me here—trusted me with his private spot. Could he be feeling the heat between us as I did? My breathing became ragged. My nipples ached with a hardness my naïve mind couldn't deny. My entire body yearned for Stephan.

"You have no idea what hunger you incite in me, Hannah." His breath fell against my forehead as he drew me forward until my hips collided with his groin. "Your thoughts drive me mad with the need to possess you."

I stumbled on his statement, but any attempt to understand it vanished when his hand wrapped in my hair and he drew me to his lips. I closed my eyes. Unable to breathe, I prayed my pounding pulse wouldn't explode with the turbulent flames of anticipation burning me.

His lips caressed mine and his tongue tasted my mouth, tracing the contours before foraying to my tongue. I swallowed his groan, thinking it more of a growl. My arms wrapped around him.

The kiss was unexpected and unlike any of the wayward advances village men had made—not that many had tried. I followed his lead and clung to him, my body burning with a need I didn't understand or know how to sate. All I knew was Stephan would absolve me from my raging desires.

His kiss grew more demanding, more consuming. I relished his body crushed against mine. Heat spread through my legs as he lifted my dress. I moaned when he guided me toward the tree until my back was pressed against it. His hand ran up my thigh while his mouth claimed mine.

His other hand rubbed an aching nipple through my dress.

I longed to strip and feel his fingers on me there. A growl echoed around us and mingled with my gasp as his fingers found my pussy.

Hot lips moved to my ear. The huskiness of his voice rumbled through me. "You're so wet for me, Hannah."

www.samhainpublishing.com

CPSIA information can be obtained at www.ICGtesting.com
Printed in the USA
LVOW081659200212

269551LV00007B/16/P